DOGWOOD
PRESS

CHERRY BOMB

Susan Cushman

A NOVEL

SUSAN CUSHMAN

DOGWOOD
PRESS

Library of Congress Control Number: 2017934833

Printed in the United States of America

Author photo by Maude Schuyler-Clay
Cover photo ©Sergey Basin/123rf.com
Brick wall ©ensup/123rf.com
Icon background © apostrophe
Mary of Egypt icon painting by Susan Cushman
Cherry Bomb graffiti by Susan Cushman

First Dogwood Press edition: August 2017

Disclaimer: *Cherry Bomb* is a novel in which fictional characters
interact with historical figures. These interactions and the accom-
panying dialogue are products of the author's imagination and not
to be construed as real. Some events in the lives of the historical
figures have also been fictionalized to enhance the story. More details about this can be found in the Author's Note at the end of the
book. In the case of the fictional characters, any resemblance to
persons living or dead is entirely coincidental.

DOGWOOD PRESS

DOGWOOD PRESS
P.O. Box 5958 • Brandon, MS 39047
www.dogwoodpress.com

For Bill, my husband of forty-seven years,
who has been patient and supportive
as I have pursued my dreams.
My journey has been messy—like Mare's—
and I know I'm not easy to live with.
I love you.

ACKNOWLEDGMENTS

It's been a long journey—seven years since the inception of *Cherry Bomb*. There are so many people to thank. I'll start at the beginning. My early inspiration came from Cassandra King, whom I met at the 2006 Southern Festival of Books in Memphis. She inspired me to write "my story," although at the time I thought it would become a memoir.

Once I turned to fiction, the first readers of early chapters of the novel were my fellow participants at the Yoknapatawpha Summer Writers Workshop in Oxford, Mississippi, and our leaders, Scott Morris and M.O. "Neal" Walsh, who believed in me from the beginning. Also my friends in the Yoknapatawpha Writers Group, especially Doug McCain and Herman King. And then Suzanne Hudson and Joe Formichella gave me feedback at an early reading in Fairhope, Alabama. And so I kept writing.

Julie Cantrell, Ellen Ann Fentress, and Sally Thomason read the complete manuscript at various stages, and my first editor, Mary Ann Bowen, was crucial in guiding me in the right direction. Neil White and Corey Mesler were valuable advisors. My Memphis writing group gave support, especially Ellen Morris Prewitt, Suzanne Henley, and Blake Burr. Close friends who encouraged me throughout the journey include Deb Mashburn, Daphne Davenport, and Katherine Thames. My sweet and smart husband Bill, who read an early draft, was moved to tears, which moved me to persevere.

And so I kept going through a grueling agent search (parting ways with one who had a different vision for the book) and multiple rewrites, and finally landed in the hands of my gifted and patient editor/publisher, Joe Lee at Dogwood Press in Brandon, Mississippi. I felt I had come full circle—back to my home state. And finally, my talented daughter-in-law, See Cushman, worked her graphic design magic on my icon of Saint Mary of Egypt, who is now weeping on the back cover of the book.

As Rodney Atkins says, *these are my people*. Thank you to each and every one of you.

PROLOGUE

1981

MARE'S BACKPACK CLINKED as she ducked in and out of the pre-dawn shadows. An unusually cool summer breeze rustled the low-hanging crape myrtle branches along the sidewalk. Pausing to rearrange the aerosol cans and wrap them with t-shirts to silence them, she pulled up her hood and looked down the street. No one there. Storefronts were still dark in this southern city of a quarter million people. Macon, Georgia, felt big compared to the smaller towns of Mare's childhood. But not so big that she couldn't find her way through the mostly abandoned city streets on her clandestine missions.

Rounding a corner, she heard scuffling and discovered a homeless man huddled behind a dumpster, the contents of his life stuffed into a shopping cart. His cough disturbed a sleeping cat that sprung from underneath his frayed blanket. An empty bottle rolled onto the sidewalk. Mare hurried by as a light came on in a nearby window.

Taking a nervous breath of the crisp morning air, Mare breathed in the aroma of cinnamon rolls from the bakery across the street. When had she eaten last? She put the thought out of her mind and found her target a few blocks away: Family and Children Services. The parking lot was empty. She moved quickly, choosing a spot near the entrance. She broke the lights on either side of the doorway with one of her cans. She worked swiftly but with deliberation, needing the protection of the quickly fading darkness. She opened a can of black spray paint and stared at the brick wall in front of her.

What a rush.

She shook the can vigorously and felt the familiar jolt of electricity as she heard the metal ball bouncing around inside. The feeling was akin, she felt, to her lungs finally opening after being clamped shut for years. Removing the cap, she approached the wall, took aim, and pressed the valve, releasing a fine spray mist with all the skill of a trained artist.

For the last few weeks, most of her pieces had been simple designs or just tags. Today's message would be more complex. She had spent months working it out; now she would share it with the world. Well, at least with Macon. The reporter for the *Macon News* would take care of the rest. After Mare had come to town and started throwing up her graffiti, Margaret Adams had launched her own personal quest—not only to expose Mare's work, but also to expose Mare. Mare had evaded her grasp so far, moving from one part of town to another, sleeping here and there, always carrying her backpack with her and leaving nothing at the scene except the art itself. Adams had featured several of Mare's pieces in the *News*, complete with photographs. Graffiti was not common in the Southeast; the reporter couldn't leave it alone. *Who is this tagger, and where does he live?* Adams opined in print. It amused Mare that the reporter thought the artist was a guy.

She always tossed her empty cans into random dumpsters after each hit, careful not to leave a trail. She must not be arrested—it absolutely couldn't happen—and she *had* to throw up these next two pieces. Blue lights and sirens approached just as she was getting started, though. Diving behind some shrubs that bordered the parking lot, she held her breath. Two squad cars flew through the blinking orange lights at a nearby intersection, oblivious to her crime. Wiping the sweat from her brow with her sleeve, she crawled out from behind the shrubs and quickened her pace as the sun began to light the wall and wake the town.

Her signature character—a little girl with big, empty eyes and no mouth—would be featured in this piece. She outlined the image with black, painted the hair yellow, and overlaid the face with orange. Bloody drops fell from the red heart painted on the character's chest. The child's eyes gazed upward to a large shadow-like creature. The character soon took shape; it was a man, hovering over the girl. The image of the girl faded below her heart, as if her lower body was disappearing.

She's been disappearing for years, hasn't she?

Mare felt tears as she viewed the image, biting her lower lip. "Screw you," she hissed, flipping off the shadow-man.

She heard a car engine and looked at her watch. Almost 6:30. Just enough time for her tag—a red cherry with yellow rays emanating from a black stem and the word BOMB in red bubble letters, outlined with black. She could imagine tomorrow's headline in the *News:*

CHERRY DROPS ANOTHER BOMB!

PART ONE

ONE

MARE ALWAYS WONDERED why her father named the farm Heaven's Gate. The few times she had seen the gate at the end of the dirt road on which she lived, it didn't look like it led to Heaven. But then again, she had no way of knowing for sure, since she wasn't allowed off the property. Her whole world, as long as she could remember, consisted of the rundown trailer where she lived with her family and the small farm they worked with others in nearby trailers.

Heaven's Gate was a commune in central Georgia much like many hippie communities that had popped up all over the country in the 1960s and '70s. In 1964 a drifter named Scott Henry had managed to scrounge up some money to lease the property and gather a small but loyal group of disenchanted teenagers around him, including Mare's mother, Grace. Grace was just one of Scott's "wives." Scott kept these wives pregnant and dependent upon him for everything, including drugs. He and Grace had three children: Mare and her younger brothers, Phoenix and Jagger.

Grace was barely more than a child herself when she came under the spell of Scott's charms. Her natural beauty—ash blond hair, hazel eyes and long, lithe legs flowing from her budding young curves—won Scott's attention and she soon became his favorite. But his treatment of Grace turned her into an unfit mother.

"Mare, precious," her mother would say in rare moments of sobriety, "come over here and give me a kiss."

Mare was twelve and took what she could get. Snuggled up against her mother on those nights when her father was elsewhere—spreading the love around the farm—she dreamed of running away with her mother. She lived in constant fear.

"Father scares me," she whispered. "He touches me, down here, when he takes me to the temple. He makes me hurt. Does he hurt Jagger and Phoenix like that? And the other farm children?"

Mare's mother only held her closer. She had no words for her daughter, only tears.

Even as a child, Mare knew she would never be as weak as her mother. She would never let a man hurt her children. Not even if he said he was God's messenger.

• • •

"Come with me to the temple, Mare," her father said as he reached for her hand.

He was older than her mother—in his early thirties—and his six-foot frame commanded respect, or at least fear. His shoulder-length coffee-colored hair was unkempt and his broad shoulders bulged from the old cutoff t-shirts he usually wore at work on the farm. He rarely bathed and the hint of patchouli oil did little to mask his odor. His voice was deep and authoritative. Only rarely did Grace speak up on Mare's behalf.

"What do you need the child for tonight, Scott? I need help with the dishes. It's late and—"

"Grace, you know. Mare has a special calling. Just clean up the kitchen yourself. Help your mother, boys."

The boys were used to helping, although they were only eight and ten. They worked in the vegetable gardens during the day when they weren't tending the small livestock population or helping with repairs. Everything seemed to be falling apart, including the barn, which Scott and the other men had converted into a makeshift temple.

"I need something, Scott." She begged him with her eyes. "You know, to make me feel better."

"Get the boys to bed. When I come home I'll give you something."

"Can I have it now? *Please*?" She bit her lip and tugged on her husband's sleeve.

"Not until the boys are asleep, Grace. Let's go, Mare."

Mare didn't know exactly what her mother needed, but she knew her father held a god-like power over all of them. And not just her mother and brothers—Scott had other wives who were older than Grace. Some of them already had children from their teenage years when they arrived at the farm. These wives were needy, too, though, and Scott tired of them quickly.

Walking through the dust along the road that led to the barn, Mare pulled away from her father to pick a wildflower. Its bright lavender petals and yellow center contrasted with the brown farmland, which was dotted mostly with weeds. "What kind of flower is this, Father?"

"It's just a weed, Mare. Why are you bothering with that?"

"I thought I would take it with us to the temple. God would like it, wouldn't He?"

Her father grabbed her hand and hastened their pace. Mare felt a knot in her stomach as they approached the temple. It was an old, gray, weather-beaten barn that still held the stench of animals from years past. The smell, mixed with her father's body odor, was nauseating to Mare, but she tried to smile as she placed the flower on the bench next to them as they sat down.

It wasn't the first evening like this one, when her father took her to the temple alone. The first time, she had felt special, chosen. He held her in his lap and prayed, caressing her gently. But soon the caressing turned into fondling. And on this night he told her she was ready for a special ceremony.

"Take off your clothes, Mare."

"In church? But, Father—"

"It's what God wants, child. It's the highest form of worship."

He laid a white sheet on the dirt floor and told her to lie down on it. She thought she would die the first time he entered her— the physical pain was unbearable. After he finished, he took the bloodstained sheet, held it up toward the altar, and said a prayer. Then he told her that God was pleased with her sacrifice.

Sometime later Mare tried to tell her mother about it, but her father kept Grace so drugged most of the time she seemed oblivious to what was happening to her daughter. All the children at the farm were homeschooled (if one could call their meager instruction an education) and had very little contact with the outside world, so there was no one else to tell, nowhere her voice could be heard.

Then one night her father told her it would be their last ceremony. "God wants us to come to Heaven, Mare. To be with Him."

"But Father, I thought we didn't go to Heaven until we died."

"God works in mysterious ways, child. Now quit talking and take off your clothes."

After he had finished with her and walked her back to the trailer, Mare lay awake all night, waiting for God to take her to Heaven. Just before dawn, her mother came to her room.

"Mare, wake up, honey," she whispered fiercely. "We're leaving."

Mare blinked a couple of times, then looked out the trailer's window into the darkness. "Is Father going with us? And Phoenix and Jagger?"

"They're at the temple, preparing for a special meeting with God later this morning."

"Oh, wow … is this when we're all going to Heaven?"

"No. Yes—I mean, your father has told everyone that we're going, but—"

"But, what? It's not true, is it?"

"No, honey, it's not. Now get dressed, quickly!"

Something's bad wrong about this. "What about my clothes?"

"I've already packed them. Hurry!"

Mare looked around their trailer, searching for her few belongings—an old doll, a small coloring book, and some crayons her mother had gotten her on a recent trip to town for groceries (Mare wasn't allowed to go with her mother on those trips). The items were her treasures from the outside world, and Grace nodded as she bundled them into a pillowcase.

She held her mother's hand as they slipped out of the trailer and ran down the dirt road toward the edge of the farm. It was still dark, but the sun would be up soon, Mare knew. Lights were beginning to come on in the other trailers. Birds offering their morning songs were the only sounds other than their footsteps on the gravel. Her mother kept looking over her shoulder as they ran for the entrance. A truck topped the hill just as they climbed over the gate.

"Stop! Please!" Grace called out, waving her right arm high in the air. Mare, frightened now, was clinging to her skirt like a girl much younger than twelve. The truck stopped, and they climbed into the cab. The driver was an old man in coveralls, but he struck Mare as kind. She'd never seen him before.

"Where are you going, ma'am?"

"Anywhere. Just away from here." Grace looked out the window at the sign above the entrance to the farm. "Quickly, please."

As they drove away, blue lights appeared behind them. Grace gasped as men with guns jumped out of their cars and emergency vans moved into view at the gate. One of the men busted down the gate and the vehicles drove onto the property, sirens now blaring. Transfixed, Mare leaned out the window of the truck and looked back at the scene.

Grace pulled her back inside and hugged her tightly. "It's okay, Mare. It's going to be okay."

As the farm disappeared behind them, Mare looked ahead into the view of the truck's headlights on the deserted country road. "Where are we going, Mother?"

"Somewhere safe. Just rest now."

Laying her head against her mother's shoulder, Mare tried to keep her eyes open. The sparsely-placed houses drew her attention. Each house was bordered by trees and a barn. She wondered what kind of families lived there. Were those barns their temples? As they drove along and eventually hit a two-lane blacktop road, she watched farmers heading out to their fields in the sunrise and children carrying books in their arms as they walked out to wait for the school bus. She had heard about the schools that other children went to—children who didn't take their lessons at home. Would she go to one of those schools now? Where would she and her mother live? She looked at Grace on the seat next to her—her mother was biting her lip—and decided not to ask questions yet. Mare looked up in time to see a sign in the ground on the side of the road which read FORSYTH, GEORGIA.

"Right there ... please take this turn," Grace said urgently.

The truck driver took the exit. "Where now, lady?"

"It's just a few miles, I think. Just keep going on this road, please."

Maybe ten minutes passed, Mare figured, before they hit the edge of town. Another mile or so later they were downtown. Grace pointed, and the old man pulled up along the curb of a two-story brick building. Grace told Mare to hop out, and Mare opened the door and stepped down onto a cracked sidewalk. Grace got out, then turned to the truck driver.

"Wait here, please. I'll only be a few minutes."

"Wait? For what?" he muttered.

Mare looked at him carefully. Gray hair framed his face and crow's feet spread from his eyes. She wondered in that instant what he did for a living—was he in some way connected to Heaven's Gate? That didn't seem possible, but ...

"I thought this was where I was taking you, lady. I got a schedule to keep."

Grace looked at Mare, then back at the man. "Just wait, please."

He hesitated, then nodded and put the truck in park. Grace took Mare up the steps to the front door.

"Sit still until I'm out of sight," she said quietly. "Then go inside. Someone will help you."

Mare felt a ripple of fear down her back. "But Mother, where are you going?"

"I'm going to find us a place. I need to get clean, Mare. I need to learn how to be a good mother so I can come back for you." She kissed Mare, held her close for a long moment, and hurried down the steps—and back into the truck. Now Mare felt real terror at the thought of being abandoned. Her mouth fell open as she stared at her mother, but Grace looked straight ahead. Then the truck pulled away from the curb.

A moment later it was gone.

• • •

Mare sat for a minute, maybe more, thinking this was all a big mistake, that the truck would suddenly come barreling back up and her mother would yell for her to join them. But it didn't. It was early morning, the parking lot by the building was empty, and not a soul was in sight. Mare tried to open the front door but it was locked, so she waited on the steps. Eventually she felt herself growing sleepy and leaned back against the door. The next thing she knew a car pulled up. She opened her eyes and watched as a woman got out, shut her door, and came striding up.

"And just who are you?" the woman said gently. She looked older than Grace but not as old as the man who'd driven them from the farm.

"My mother brought me here," Mare said, her voice thick with sleep. "She said someone would take care of me. She'll come back for me when she's better."

"Where do you live, honey?"

"At Heaven's Gate."

The woman nodded and unlocked the door. Then she took Mare's hand and led her into the building. The sign above the door said FORSYTH DEPARTMENT OF CHILD SERVICES.

Inside, the woman took her into a room with couches and chairs and toys, where Mare was given cereal and juice. Something called *Sesame Street* was playing on the television. Mare had never seen a TV program—television was forbidden at the farm. She sat and stared, trance-like. Another woman, maybe a little younger and with a long pony-tail down her back, came to sit with her while the first woman talked on the telephone in the adjacent office. Mare could see her through the open door but was drawn back to Ernie and Bert and Big Bird.

Mare stared into space after a while. She wondered what her mother was doing and where she was going. Grace had looked her in the eye, hugged her, and promised she would return for her, so Mare had no doubt she would. But when?

"... mass suicide at Heaven's Gate, that cult out in the county."

This got Mare's attention. She opened her eyes and looked toward the office, where two uniformed police officers were talking in hushed tones to the woman who'd let Mare inside. The woman covered her mouth.

"Seventy-three dead, including the leader."

The woman stood, tears in her eyes. And pointed Mare out to the policemen.

• • •

"Uncle Miles" and "Aunt Sue" had a small patch of land in Forsyth. Their names were on the list of folks willing to take in orphans and abandoned kids, so Mare ended up under their roof as their foster child. Aunt Sue had seemed kind enough when the DCS lady interviewed the couple, though Uncle Miles mostly kept his mouth shut and his hands in his overalls—until they got back to his house. Even so, things were calm enough during the days; he was usually sleeping off the previous night's drinking while Aunt Sue was doing alterations at the dry cleaners. Mare would roam freely around the property after doing her chores, which included feeding the chickens when she first moved to her new home at age twelve, and cooking most of their meals as she got older. The work wasn't any harder than it had been at the farm, but she really missed her mother and brothers at night and often cried herself to sleep.

A good part was attending the county school. Mare's favorite class was art. She would lose herself in the magic of watching her thoughts come to life as her hand guided the crayons across the sheets of manila paper. As she got older she used charcoal and eventually paint to create scenes from what she later learned was her subconscious—something within was driving her hand.

But her teachers never seemed to notice the message she was trying to convey as she drew and then painted the same scenes over and over: usually a girl with big eyes and no mouth, sometimes with tears or even blood flowing down her face. Often a large, dark creature lurked in the background or in the air above the girl. Sometimes the creature had only a large head and his arms were raised in the air. At other times she painted the full body of a man standing over the girl. Her drawings looked frightening to her, but she felt better when she drew them, less afraid somehow. At the end of class she would sneak extra paper and pencils into her backpack and take those stolen treasures home with her, continuing to sketch under the cover of darkness in her room.

When she was almost sixteen she signed up for art classes at the community center—something to look forward to during the long hot Georgia summer. But one day Uncle Miles found her hidden stash of artwork in her room.

"What the hell is this?" He stumbled out of the house into the yard, the smell of Jack Daniels and tobacco on his breath, with a handful of her sketches in his hand. He threw her drawings into a barrel, saturated them with kerosene, lit another unfiltered Winston, and tossed the match into the barrel. It set her hopes on fire and silenced her only voice.

"Trash, that's what it is," he slurred. "Monsters. All eyes and no mouths. And these weird bodies like ... hell, I don't know what they are! What were you thinking?"

"Uncle Miles, those were very important to me—"

"Here's what you're gonna think from now on: about doing your *chores*. Helping your Aunt Sue. Earning your keep. No more stupid drawings, you hear me? And no art classes at the community center this summer!"

Watching her sketches float into the sky—bits of ashes rising up to Heaven—Mare wished she could fly away with them. She felt her heart being ripped out of her body, as she did on those dark nights when Uncle Miles stole the remains of her battered childhood. She knew what was coming and curled up on the floor in the corner of her room when she heard him cussing the stack of magazines she always left just inside the door.

"Dammit, Mare!" He would lose his balance and fall onto her bed, the smell of the booze and tobacco strong on his breath. "Get your butt over here, girl. You know you want it, you little slut." He might as well have torched her body, too, what was left of it when he finished with her.

But one day hope came to her from an unexpected source.

"Turn that damned thing down!"

That was Uncle Miles, slamming his bedroom door and stumbling back to his bed—he was so hungover he hadn't gotten near her today. Aunt Sue had gone into town for groceries. Mare scurried across the bare living room floor and lowered the volume of the television. She plopped back down on the couch, moving aside her cold TV dinner.

Her eyes never left the screen as Blondie performed "Rapture" with Fab 5 Freddy. In the final scene, lead singer Debbie Harry was dancing along the street. A Native American, Uncle Sam, and a goat made appearances in the video. It was 1981 and this was the first hip-hop video on MTV. Mare was smitten with Debbie Harry and mesmerized by the rap music, but it was graffiti artists Lee Quinones and Jean-Michael Basquiat who caught her attention as they painted on the walls in the background. She recognized that artist—*Quinones*—she'd seen his tags somewhere. Art students at the high school took field trips to museums in Macon and Atlanta, but Uncle Miles hadn't allowed her to study art since he had discovered her drawings.

Why do those images look familiar?

When the video was over, Mare grabbed an apple from the kitchen counter and walked outside. It was an unusually hot day for April, even in Georgia. She walked down the dirt road and found shade along a tree-lined stream. Wiping the apple juice from her mouth with the back of her hand, she heard a train coming and looked across the field at the freight cars. The afternoon sun cast a glare across the grass, blurring the images moving past on the sides of the cars. As the train slowed, the wheels ground to a stop with the sound of steel on steel. Mare covered her ears with her hands.

But then the images came into view. She remembered why the pictures on MTV looked familiar. Throwing the apple core into the stream, she ran toward the tracks. Car after car was covered with murals. There were anti-war slogans alongside apocalyptic images of grotesque creatures and guns and helicopters ... next to peaceful scenes of a green earth and children and flowers and peace signs. She saw the name LEE in bubble letters on one car and recognized it from the video.

Oh my God!

The moment was her epiphany, the instant Mare knew she had found a voice for her story. But how could she paint on railroad cars? The trains didn't stop overnight in Forsyth. They barely slowed for the sparse traffic at the one crossing in town. The pieces and tags in the video were on the walls of the buildings in the city. *The city is New York.* Forsyth was anything but a city. Could she go into Macon—what was it, twenty-five miles away? Macon was no New York City, but she just might have an audience there, someone to hear her story.

What could she use for paint, though? She would need the little money she had saved for bus fare into Macon. The art students at school used spray cans for stage scenery. They left their markers and brushes out after class every day, but she couldn't afford those.

She kicked at the ground. This felt so real. And so out of reach.

• • •

One day she watched an MTV television interview with graffiti artists who talked about how to make homemade ink from carbon paper and lighter fluid. Mare smiled to herself. She knew how to steal those things from school and home.

"You can use grocery store ink," a young graffiti artist said, demonstrating how to put purplish ink into a refillable marker. "The good thing is, it's permanent. I was bagging groceries and could rack some of the stuff when the manager wasn't looking." Mare grinned again. Every step of the process held a clandestine, almost seductive allure for her. Especially the stealing.

"It's cheaper just to shred carbon paper. Like this." The artist ripped the paper into strips, filling an old paint can. "Then you mix it with alcohol. Or lighter fluid." He poured the liquid into the can and stirred it with a metal spatula. "After it sits for a while, you strain it. Like this." He poured it through a strainer.

Next, he stuffed old aerosol deodorant containers with socks and filled them with the homemade ink. He finished with a demonstration in the television studio, spraying a tag on a wall covered with butcher paper.

• • •

Mare gathered supplies over the next few weeks and hid them in the old shed Uncle Miles had used for making moonshine before Monroe County legalized liquor. Finally, she was ready to make her own ink. She found it surprisingly simple. But she wanted to use colors like Icy Grape, Jungle Green, and Red Devil, so she racked some cans from the art room at school before the janitor cleaned the place for the summer.

She turned sixteen in May and got a summer job at the hardware store. It was easy to sneak a can here and there without anyone noticing, although she felt bad about it. Old Mr. Sanders had been so nice to her.

"How's your Aunt Sue doing?" he asked one day.

"She's okay."

"I haven't seen her at the dry cleaners lately. Has she been sick?"

"No, it's Uncle Miles. He's needs her help at the house, is all. Especially with me working in town."

Mr. Sanders nodded as if he understood and didn't ask anything further. Uncle Miles was on disability, claiming a bum leg from a construction accident. The doctor had signed off on it to keep Aunt Sue and Mare from starving.

Mare kept a low profile, spending the summer working on the graffiti sketchbook that the guys in the MTV interview had called a *piecebook*. She outlined ideas and worked out designs, dreaming of the day she could bring them to life in Macon. These were the only times she was happy—lost in the world of graffiti art, and learning to tell her story.

She really liked the Old School writers, like Blade and Comet with their blockbuster letters, and Phase 2, who invented bubble letters. She had pages of bubbled tags, on which she practiced names in several styles and colors. Her goal was to write graffiti on a couple of buildings on a side street in Macon by the end of the summer. The university kids would be arriving back in town just in time to admire her bombs. In those last few weeks in Forsyth, the scenes from her early abstract drawings that Uncle Miles had burned cropped back up as she sketched. Most were simple black-and-whites and darker than ever. The circles under the girl's eyes were deeper than those in her childhood attempts; some of her figures now had mouths, but tiny ones—closed, afraid. Like she'd felt all her life.

Mare didn't just want to do throw-ups, the simple bubble letter phrases that were commonplace on the trains she studied as they sped through town. She wanted to tell stories through murals, known as *pieces* in the graffiti world. But how could she do it if she only spent a couple of hours at a time in the city? And how could she sneak out over and over without Uncle Miles and Aunt Sue catching her? She was too young to be emancipated legally.

Maybe it was time to just run away and live on the streets.

• • •

The window air conditioner hummed loudly and dropped moisture on the floor in the living room where Mare sat one night in August, waiting for the light in the back bedroom to click off. In another ten minutes Uncle Miles and Aunt Sue were asleep. Mare hurried out the back door and down the road with paint supplies in her backpack and a few clothes and an old comforter in her duffle bag. It was fifteen minutes to the bus stop. The locusts almost drowned out the voice in her head that said, *You're crazy. They'll catch you and put you in juvie.* But how, Mare almost said aloud, would that be worse than her current living arrangements?

It was almost ten-thirty when she reached the stop. She waited alone in the quiet, almost eerie night, and was relieved when the city bus came into view even as its headlights blinded Mare momentarily. Ignoring the driver's quizzical look, she found a seat near the front, where the lights from the dash gave off a safe, warm glow in the darkness. Only a handful of other passengers filled the rows behind her. She found herself glancing over her shoulder frequently during the forty-minute trip. It would become an ingrained habit over the next few weeks in Macon, where she would learn the side streets and back alleys as well as she knew Forsyth.

Arriving in the protective darkness of midnight, she immediately began searching the vacant walls of the buildings, selecting her "canvas." This task took priority over even her basic needs for food and a place to sleep. By early dawn she had chosen a brick wall near a coffee shop and had thrown up her first piece to let the town know she had arrived. It was a simple, two-color piece: a red cherry outlined in black with canary yellow sparks emanating from its stem, and her tag, "Cherry Bomb," in puffy black letters in a cloud above the drawing. Stylized red droplets bled from the letters onto the cherry.

It was difficult working with the fat tips of the aerosol cans—hadn't she heard somewhere how to cut lines, make them thinner?—and she was a little disappointed; the tag wasn't as polished as the sketch in her piecebook. Maybe she could find cans with smaller tips somewhere in Macon. She could hardly wait to write a real piece, but she was so exhausted from the night's adventure that she fell asleep on a nearby bench.

Not long after, she woke to bright sunlight, the smell of coffee, and the sound of Kim Carnes' "Bette Davis Eyes" streaming from a college kid's Walkman as he hurried down the sidewalk. He adjusted his backpack and looked at his watch, paying no attention to her.

TWO

"**G**ET DRESSED, GIRLS, we're going to the Museum of Modern Art for Elaine's birthday."

Elaine was turning nine. "What will we see there, Mother?"

"A very important exhibition. It's Pablo Picasso. Several hundred of his paintings."

And there were. His massive painting, *Guernica*, held Elaine spellbound. Eleven feet tall and over twenty-five feet wide, the mural covered an entire wall. In the center a horse was falling over in agony as a javelin ran through its middle. The horse landed on a dismembered soldier with a severed hand holding a sword that appeared to sprout a flower. Elaine's little sisters were horrified by the painting, but Elaine was drawn to it—even with the terror it illustrated.

Victims of a bombing were thrown everywhere. On the left side of the painting, a wide-eyed bull stood over a woman grieving her dead child in her arms. At first Elaine stood close enough that she could almost reach out and touch it. But then she backed up across the room to get a fuller view of the massive piece.

"What do you like about it, Elaine?" In her moments of near-sanity, her mother, Marie, was a wonderful teacher.

"The power. Like something I've seen in my dreams. The people and animals don't look exactly—they look, well, *more* than real."

Her mother smiled. "The word is *surreal*, Elaine. You have a good eye. Maybe you will be an artist one day."

Elaine looked back at the painting, relishing her mother's praise as much as the brilliant art she was observing.

Growing up in Brooklyn in the titillating 1920s, depressed '30s, and war-torn '40s, Elaine learned early on to take care of herself and her sisters. Her father had left after her youngest sister was born. Her mother was always entertaining eccentric friends, giving parties where the costumes and the liquor flowed like silk. The guests played with Elaine and her sisters like they were pets—dressing them up and taking turns with them in the upstairs bedrooms. Their mother's cloche hats and chemises swallowed their tiny frames. Elaine's straight black hair was perfectly bobbed. Sometimes it was fun to play with her mother's beads and faux furs, but the fun was only a prelude to the dark sexual activities that followed—often involving both men and women. Elaine would imagine escaping as she listened to Ella Fitzgerald's voice lilting up the stairs from the living room, crooning "Bye Bye Blackbird."

One day a neighbor blew the whistle and her mother was arrested. Behind bars, Marie's eccentricities evolved into full-blown mental illness. She spent several years in a psychiatric center in Queens in the 1930s, leaving Elaine and her sisters in the care of their uncle, a frequent guest at his sister's parties. Uncle Charles wasn't a much better caregiver than their mother had been. He was just more discreet.

He finally died of a heart attack, and the girls were on their own by the time their mother got out of the institution. Elaine lost no time getting back out to the museums where her mother had introduced her to the work of the great abstract masters.

The first time she saw Jackson Pollock's work—at his first solo show in 1943—her affinity for art grew stronger. Even as a young woman, she understood Pollock's talent for revealing unconscious moods. Staring at "The Moon Woman Cuts the Circle" at the Guggenheim when she was in her early twenties, Elaine could feel the connection between the moon and the feminine psyche. A thick mixture of paint and other materials—impasto—gave his work a three-dimensional quality. Pouring, dripping, and scraping paint added spontaneity and a sense of urgency. She could hardly keep herself from reaching out and touching the surface; she wanted to feel the texture of the work. All of this drew Elaine into Pollock's world, and she began to look for opportunities to study art.

With no financial backing, she looked for legal ways to make money with her body (the only currency she knew how to trade). Walking down 34th Street one afternoon, she saw an advertisement for models posted outside the Leonardo da Vinci Art School. Her body was perfect—childlike with only a hint of womanly curves.

Walking into the studio to inquire, she met Richard Joyce, one of the artists employed by the New Deal's Works Progress Administration to teach art classes at the school. He smiled at her heavy makeup and her pompadour, a style usually reserved for older women. Her calf-length shirtwaist dress from a thrift store did little to disguise the terrified girl within.

"So, you'd like to model?"

"Yes. Yes, sir."

"You're obviously young, but you have good strong features. Are you willing to pose nude?"

"Of course," Elaine said.

"And why do you want to model?"

"I want to study art and I don't have money for it."

"Ah, another starving artist in the making. Perfect. Come back next Monday morning at eleven."

• • •

When Elaine arrived at the studio, she expected a room full of students. Instead, there was only Richard Joyce.

"Where is the class?"

"Oh, there's no class today. I want to do some preliminary sketches to show the students next week."

Elaine shot him a wary look.

"Don't worry. I'll pay you the same," Joyce said. "If you're good, I'll consider using you for my personal work. Go into the storage room over there and get ready. There's a robe on the hook behind the door."

As she removed her dress and underthings, she suddenly felt herself back at her mother's parties and questioned her decision to model for this man. But she needed the money. Wrapping the robe snugly around her body, she took a deep breath and came out into the studio. Joyce didn't even look up from the easel where he was gathering his materials. He simply pointed to a couch. "Just sit there. I'll position you."

His seeming disinterest gave Elaine courage. Dropping the robe, she sat down and reclined on her side, her right elbow propped on the arm of the divan and her legs stretched out, one on top of the other. Her eyes never left Joyce. He hesitated before approaching her.

"Are you sure you've never done this before?"

Her confidence had returned. "You mean have I taken my clothes off for a man? Sure. But not for an artist."

Joyce moved to gently position her arms and hands. He turned her face to lift her chin slightly, and placed his hand on the top of her thigh.

Maybe I was wrong—it's all men really want, isn't it?

But then he surprised her.

"I'm just going to move your top leg forward a bit. There, bend your knee. Let it fall on the couch in front of your other leg. Good. Sometimes it's better to leave something to the imagination."

His professionalism was disarming. No one had ever touched her like this before.

Joyce sketched fairly quickly, moving in and out from behind his easel, sometimes holding his fist in front of his nose—thumb up—to get the proportions right. Elaine never moved. After forty-five minutes he stopped.

"Do you need a break?"

"No, I'm fine."

He sketched for another forty-five minutes. She could feel his eyes on each part of her body, but it didn't feel sexual. It felt like she was contributing to something bigger than her small, insignificant self—it felt like art. When the hour and a half was up, Joyce stepped away from the canvas, crossed his arms over his chest, and looked back and forth between the sketch and the model.

"We're done for today," he said. "You can go now."

"What about my pay?"

"Stop by my desk in the front room after you get dressed. I'll have it ready for you."

"May I see the drawing?"

"Sure. Come have a look."

She put on the robe and walked over to the easel. What she saw both surprised her and stirred something new in her. The woman in the sketch only faintly resembled Elaine, but the contours and shading were flawless. The lines were precise. No effort had been made to blend the contrasting black and gray areas.

"What do you think?"

"I—I'm not sure. It's not quite what I expected."

"It's not meant to be realistic, Elaine. I've been studying the Surrealists—especially Miró—and also the Ab Ex guys right here in New York."

"My mother took me to see Picasso and Pollock, but I don't think I've heard of Ab Ex," she admitted, embarrassed by her ignorance.

"Abstract Expressionists. Do you know the work of Willem de Kooning?"

She shook her head.

Joyce laughed gently. "It's okay. You're not even a student yet. Modeling is a good introduction."

It was the easiest money Elaine had earned in her young life. She left the studio awakened to the world of visual art—and with a huge crush on Richard Joyce. A fire had been lit inside her that could not be quenched. She became a student at The da Vinci School where she began her formal training as an artist. Joyce had introduced her to a world she didn't know existed, and within a year she moved on to study with Marshall Rainey at American Artists. They were lovers—she always lost herself in these men—but Rainey lost her at a party when he introduced her to another artist.

"Elaine, I'd like you to meet Willem de Kooning. The greatest painter in the country."

• • •

Willem de Kooning's studio, where the two of them went that same night, was the cleanest studio she had ever seen—so unlike the messy environs of most artists. Neatly painted gray floors. Pristine white walls. On a table in the corner was a phonograph he had bought for $500, back when he was only making $22 a week. In the center of the room an easel held a painting like nothing she had ever seen before.

"I'm going to call it, 'Woman.' I've been working on it for months. What do you think?"

Was Willem de Kooning really asking *her* what she thought of his work? He was already the most successful Ab Exer in the city, and she had yet to sell one painting. Hulking and vampish, the woman's ferocious grin and bulging eyes demanded attention from Elaine like a voluptuous siren circling her prey. Willem's violent, misogynistic brush strokes heightened the effect.

"It's—I don't know—powerful," Elaine managed.

"I'm going for something Paleolithic. But also modern. Reverence, and fear, too, of feminine power."

"That's a universal struggle. You're aiming pretty high."

"Would you like to study with me, Elaine? I can teach you to draw, better than those clowns over at American Artists."

And so it began. Later that year Elaine sold her first watercolor for ten dollars. It wasn't an abstract. Unlike most artists working in the Ab Ex field, Elaine loved portraits, although she brought her slashing brushstrokes from her Ab Ex work into her portraits.

The next year she moved into Willem's studio. Three years later they were married. Those were some of the highest—and lowest—times of her life. Willem adored her at first. When they took breaks from working in the studio they shared, she would lean back on the couch and say, "Bill, cigarette." He would jump to get one for her and, kneeling in front of her, he would light it and ask if she needed anything else. But the honeymoon was short-lived. Willem went off to an artists' colony in Maine, and she discovered willing partners in his absence. Those were the days of partying New York style—plenty of booze and warm bodies eager to numb themselves from the pain of their own failures. Elaine found herself pregnant a few months after her new husband's departure.

She didn't know who the father was. There had been so many encounters during Willem's absence. Looking for a way to save face and continue her career, she left New York for a six-month residency at a remote artist colony in the mountains of North Carolina. She returned with a dozen or more paintings she called her Black Mountain Series—and without the child she secretly gave birth to. A social worker from the nearby Catholic orphanage told her the baby girl would be easy to place. But Elaine wanted to keep her options open. She wouldn't release her daughter for adoption. She took the baby to the orphanage; she could visit whenever she wanted. But she never returned to see the child again. She rolled up the paintings she had produced at Black Mountain, took them back to New York, and hid them. Somehow they represented the child she had abandoned. She couldn't show them to anyone.

When Willem returned a year later, he found they had been evicted from their uptown loft. They moved into a Greenwich Village apartment and set up shop together, although they no longer shared a bed.

As Willem became more prolific, so did his affairs. Being a woman in the masculine world of art, Elaine consoled herself with her own lovers and the seductive buzz of the art scene— working for *Art News*, organizing clubs, and moving in her own direction. Figurative forms in popular culture caught her painterly eye. Her first solo exhibit, held at the 10th Street Galleries in Soho, was filled with quasi-impressionist works of sports figures. Painting athletes was so physical; she felt like she was moving with them through space as she spilled and plopped and sloshed the oil and pigment onto the canvas with forceful brush strokes. But she wanted more. Always, more.

• • •

It was 1963 when Helen Abbott walked into Elaine's studio as she was at work on her life-sized portrait of John F. Kennedy. The walls and floors were covered in photographs and short-hand sketches. Slim and still youthful at forty-five, Elaine was perched on the next-to-top rung of a ladder, struggling to get the downward slant of the President's eyelids just right. By that time Elaine and Willem's ten-year marriage was on even shakier ground; Willem could not understand her inability to trust people, and childhood secrets weren't so readily shared in those days. But his on-again, off-again affair with Helen was no secret in the small world of the West Village. Elaine justified her own affairs—especially the ones with art critics like Clement Greenberg and Thomas Hess, who championed Willem's art— by telling herself she was promoting her husband's work.

But *her* extramarital activities weren't the issue on this particular spring day in 1963. It was Willem's actions that were once again a cause for drama.

"Is it true?" Helen didn't wait for Elaine's answer. "Is Willem really moving to Long Island?"

"And what's that to you?" Elaine turned from the canvas, descended the ladder, and moved to a worktable.

"It's just awful timing. So many changes happening right now." Helen paced the studio, oblivious to the sketches she trampled. Elaine lit a cigarette and moved to pour a cup of coffee from a pot on a table in the corner. She held the cup toward Helen.

"No, thank you. How can you be so calm? What will we do without him here in the Village?"

"Don't you mean what will you do without him in your *bed*?" Elaine walked back to stand in front of her portrait-in-progress. She placed her left hand on her hip, holding the cigarette near her right shoulder, and stared at the painting. Helen stepped over to face her and slowly but purposefully placed one hand on her large, round belly.

"You thought I didn't know about you and Bill?" Elaine took a long draw on the cigarette. "So, what will you do, Helen? Run after him? That will only chase him farther away. Just stay put and hope he chooses to be part of your life."

• • •

Elaine and Willem separated. Away from his shadow she gained ground in the art world, climaxing with the installation of her portrait of President Kennedy at the Harry S. Truman Library. But after his assassination the following year, she felt that something in her had died as well. She quit painting and began teaching. Weary of the fast-paced world in New York, Elaine hoped she could give her students a chance at becoming successful artists. She became a visiting professor at Yale, in California, and even in Paris.

She had no idea her visit to the South would change her life forever.

THREE

LIFE ON THE streets of Macon, Georgia, proved to be easier than Mare had anticipated. She took to stealing right away. She racked the cans of spray paint needed for her graffiti and nabbed food at convenience stores. She often hung out at The Bean, a coffee shop frequented by kids from Mercer University. Life had aged her, so she fit in well with the coeds even at sixteen. Sometimes she pretended she was one of them.

"Hi, Mare," a waif-like young woman said in greeting from behind the counter. "Want your regular today?"

"Yeah, thanks."

"How's school?" The woman topped off Mare's coffee with lots of cream and passed it across the counter.

"Good." Mare paid for the coffee and moved to a chair by the window where the light was good for sketching. She liked to bury herself in her work for hours at a time, only stopping every now and again to get a refill on her coffee. She was in a different world when she was drawing—a world where men like her father and Uncle Miles could be transformed into harmless strokes of charcoal or lead on paper. A world where she felt safe for the first time in her life.

After an hour a woman came into the shop and sat down near her. The woman nodded and smiled. Mare continued to sketch in her piecebook. She had learned not to make eye contact with most people, but something was different about this woman—she felt safe and yet vulnerable.

"Good morning."

Mare looked up. The woman carried a large camera. She appeared to be in her thirties, with long, sandy-brown hair and oversized glasses. She wore a long-sleeve black t-shirt and black pants. She was holding a cup of espresso and a copy of *Rolling Stone*.

"Morning." The sound of Mare's own voice startled her. She had only exchanged words with store clerks for the past several days.

"Are you a student at Mercer?"

Mare nodded.

The woman looked at the sketchbook and the black smudges on Mare's hands. "Art major?"

Mare nodded again.

"I'm a photographer. You've got a great look. Would you be interested in earning some money? Posing for pictures?"

Suddenly Mare wasn't so sure about this woman. "What kind of pictures?"

"Oh, nothing kinky or anything like that. I'm a journalism photographer. I'm down from New York documenting pop culture in the South."

"So why are you interested in me?"

The woman laughed, a gentle sound. "You have no idea how interesting you are, do you?"

Mare let her guard down a bit. "What would I have to do?"

The woman handed Mare a business card which read *Anne Louise Lieberman, Photographer*. "I'm Lou. Just call me. We'll set up an appointment."

"I don't have a phone."

"Well then, how about this Saturday morning? Ten okay with you? And what did you say your name was?"

"Oh, it's Mare. I don't have any classes on Saturday. Where do I meet you?"

"I've rented a small studio apartment. Just around the corner on Ash Street. Number seven, upstairs. There's good light. Oh, and if you have any samples of your art, bring a few. Helps me get into your head. Helps me set up the shoot."

"Okay. Guess I better go. See you Saturday."

Mare felt Lou's eyes on her as she walked out of the coffee shop and headed up the street toward the campus. Once she was safely out of sight, she turned down a side street and sat on a curb. Her hands were shaking. Could she make enough money modeling to support herself? The thought had never crossed her mind. She knew she was pretty—in a way—but she wore the scars of a violent childhood.

By the time she was nine or ten she had turned to the alternative universe of art to escape the only reality she had known: the reality of ugliness, of creation turned on its head by ungrateful creatures that wanted to be gods themselves. She tried to paint her way out of her childhood nightmares by illustrating the story she could not give voice to. During art classes at the county school she attended, no matter the assignment, she drew the same image—a small girl with no mouth, her eyes large and empty. Often the girl was alone. But in some drawings a shadowy image loomed above her. Sometimes Mare drew red drops, like blood, that came from the girl's eyes, or from her heart. Her teachers feigned smiles, but none of them ever asked where her clearly provocative images might have come from. Nor had any social workers from the Department of Child Services knocked on the door of her foster parents' house during those dark years of her early adolescence.

• • •

Stirred by these thoughts, she got out her piecebook, looking for the sketch she wanted to write next. And there it was.

She waited for dusk. Then she walked to the abandoned liquor store she had scouted out the day before. The door and windows were boarded up. The large sheet of plywood over the door would be perfect for her piece. Taking a can of black paint with a skinny tip, she outlined a large bottle of Jack Daniels. Next she filled in the whiskey part with a blend of brown and yellow paint. Where the label should have been she painted a man's face, with deep-set eyes and an evil grin above his scruffy beard. Just looking at the image brought a shiver up her spine. Underneath the bottle she painted a young girl with no mouth and large, empty eyes, her torso being flattened by the bottle. Drops of red blood fell from her body.

Standing back to view her work, she looked over her shoulder to be sure no one was around. Then she quickly added her tag, tossed her cans into her backpack, and ran down the street and around the corner. She couldn't decide if the pounding noise she heard was her feet hitting the pavement or her heart beating in her chest.

A few days later at The Bean, Mare picked up a copy of *The Macon News*. She almost choked on her coffee when she read the headline: GRAFFITI DISCOVERED NEAR MERCER

CAMPUS. Trying not to appear too interested, she set the paper down for a minute, looked around, and then picked it back up ... only to see a large photograph of the piece she threw up at the liquor store, as well as a smaller one of her first tag. The reporter was Margaret Adams.

> *An unknown graffiti artist has begun bombing walls near Mercer University. The first piece was this simple tag, "Cherry Bomb." This week another painting was found—this time on an abandoned liquor store on Oglethorpe—with what appears to be a message in a bottle.*
>
> *While graffiti is rampant in New York City and other large metropolitan areas, its appearance is rare in Macon. Who is this bomber? What is his agenda?* The News *has spoken with President Godsey at Mercer. Dr. Godsey assures us that if any of his students are involved, disciplinary action will be taken.*

Mare could barely contain the smile that was trying to break out on her sleepy face. *I got their attention. They're reading my work. A few more simple pieces and I'll be ready for a serious bomb.*

• • •

Saturday morning came and Mare set off for Louise Lieberman's studio. She hid her bedroll and carried only her backpack containing her paint supplies and piecebook. Stopping to wash her face and underarms and brush her teeth in the restroom at the coffee shop, she headed to Ash Street and found Number 7. Her heart raced as she climbed the stairs and rang the doorbell, which was partially covered by the corner of a peeling AC/DC bumper sticker. The apartment was in a brick four-plex in the historic district near Mercer. Bicycles were parked on most of the wrought-iron balcony railings.

Lou opened the door and welcomed Mare inside. "Coffee?"

"Sure." Mare could smell something heavenly as they walked into the kitchen. Her stomach growled, exposing the hunger she had been ignoring. A card table and three folding chairs were the only furnishings in the kitchen. The fourth chair was visible in the otherwise bare living room, adjacent to the kitchen. Sheets covered the two windows.

"Sorry about the looks of the place." Lou nodded toward the living room. "I was doing a shoot in there last night and had to block out the street lights." She poured two cups of dark coffee and motioned at the stove. "Help yourself to a blueberry muffin. They're fresh from the oven."

"Thanks. Any milk for the coffee?"

"I think there's some in the fridge."

Mare ravished one muffin before Lou could sit down and was working on a second when Lou asked, "How long since your last meal?"

Mare hesitated. "I don't know. It's busy ... you know ... with classes and all."

Lou reached across the table and touched Mare's arm. "It's okay. You don't have to pretend with me. I'm not out to blow your cover. I only want to photograph you."

Their eyes met. Mare felt that Lou could see straight through her.

"I'm an artist, Mare. It's my job to see things, and to know people for who they are. How long have you been away from home?"

Mare looked down at her ragged low-top sneakers. The yellow gum soles were worn through. Holding her arms across her stomach, she slouched in the kitchen chair and looked away.

"Look, you don't have to tell me anything you don't want to.

You're here to model. I'll pay you for your time. How does ten dollars an hour sound?"

"Wow—I mean, that'll do." Mare tried to act cool, but that was more money than she could imagine.

"Can we start with a look into your backpack?"

Mare picked the pack up from the kitchen floor and pulled out her piecebook and a few cans of paint. When she looked up, Lou smiled and reached for a newspaper on the kitchen counter. It was folded to Margaret Adams' article about the graffiti.

"I thought it was you," Lou said.

"You won't rat me out, will you?"

"Of course not. You're an artist. But you're awfully young to be on the street alone. How did you learn graffiti?"

Mare told Lou about watching MTV videos back in Forsyth and spotting the throwups on the train.

"So, what's your plan?"

"My plan?"

"Yeah. Just going to hang out and do random graffiti throwups the rest of your life?"

"No. I've got two hit-ups I wanna do in Macon. After that, I really don't know."

Lou pursed her lips, lifting one side of her mouth into the hint of a smile. "Okay, let's get started on our shoot. We'll talk more later. Bring your piecebook into the living room."

Mare stood up and started to remove her hoodie.

"Don't take that off. I want it on for the shoot."

The living room filled with morning light as Lou removed the sheets from the windows. She set up reflector screens and draped the room with large pieces of colored cloth. When the setting satisfied her, she turned to Mare.

"Let's start with you sitting on the floor, right there. Hold your piecebook and pencil, or maybe that piece of charcoal." She tilted Mare's head, slanted the piecebook so that a hint of the work was visible, and tugged on her hoodie, revealing only one eye and letting a few strands of hair fall across her face. "There, that's perfect. Hold still now. I'll take a practice shot to test the light." Lou stood behind the tripod, pushing buttons and making adjustments. After the initial shot, she removed the camera from the tripod and began to move around the studio—sometimes standing, sometimes kneeling, and shooting Mare from different angles. "Go ahead, draw. Pretend like I'm not here. I'm shooting these at fast shutter speed with a wide aperture. It's okay if you aren't perfectly still."

Mare looked up from her work and watched Lou. "You're so graceful, like a dancer."

Smiling, Lou finished up and sat beside Mare. "My mother was a dancer. I guess it's in the genes."

Thoughts of her own mother flooded Mare's mind, as hard as she worked to block them.

"Oh, I'm sorry, Mare. I guess talking about my mother makes you sad, huh? I didn't mean—"

"No, it's okay. I try not to think about her much. Are we almost finished?"

Lou reached into a bag and brought out three ten-dollar bills and handed them to Mare. "Where are you sleeping?"

"Here and there. Now I can stay at the women's shelter. Or maybe get a room at the YWCA. I'll be fine."

"Okay. How about coming back for another session next Saturday? Mid afternoon would be good for what I have in mind."

"Sure. I'll see you then."

"Will I see more of your work in the *News* any time soon?"

Mare shrugged her shoulders and managed a tentative smile.

It was hard to leave the comfort of Lou's apartment for the realities of life on the streets, but with thirty bucks in her pocket her prospects were better. She had no intention of spending that money on a room at the Y. Tired of racking cheap cans, now she could buy some decent paint for her next project. Right after a good meal at the meat-and-three near the coffee shop.

• • •

Mare spent the following week hitting up random walls around town—nothing spectacular, but her skills were improving. It was risky business, and the adrenaline rush was her escape fuel.

"Hey *you!*"

An employee arriving early to open the Christian bookstore on Jefferson briefly gave chase. Mare ran around the corner and hid behind a garbage container. Her courage was rewarded each time another of Margaret Adams' articles appeared in the *Macon News.*

By the following Thursday she was ready to hit one of her main targets, Family and Children's Services of Macon. It was time to let them know how they had failed her, leaving her in the care of Uncle Miles when she was only twelve. She had practiced on a fence outside an abandoned warehouse to get it right. Especially the part where the girl's body gradually disappears beneath her heart. The image of the man towering over the girl was easy.

She hid the afternoon before in the back of an abandoned pickup truck across the street, watching the employees leave. She remembered how it felt to be left on the steps of a similar place by her mother. Tears blurred her vision as she watched the last of the employees drive away. Someone came walking near the truck and she ducked, burying her head in her backpack. Listening for their steps to fade away, she fell asleep. The sound of a delivery truck woke her just before dawn. She cursed to herself, needing to pee but wanting to get this done before first light, and hurried across the parking lot to the wall she had chosen.

Mare laid her piecebook on the ground as a reference and set her cans beside it. Her hands were shaking as she picked up the black paint to begin the outlines. Was it hate or hope that guided her hand as she deftly moved the aerosol can across the wall, telling the story that kept her trapped inside her own fear all these years? She worked fast, nervously looking around for cars or people who might be out for an early-morning walk.

This was her first major bomb. She finished with her tag, stood, and looked at the image until she heard a car on a nearby street. No blue lights this time, but she still ducked behind some shrubs until the car passed.

• • •

On Saturday she arrived at Lou's with copies of Margaret Adams' latest articles. "Have you seen these?" She was beaming—more like a child than a sulky teenager.

"Yes." Lou greeted Mare with a hot cup of coffee and a subdued smile. "Sit down. Have a muffin." She watched Mare stuff herself before continuing. "Mare, if I'm going to be aiding and abetting, I need to know a little more about what's behind your mission."

Mare stopped eating and looked at Lou. She washed down her last bite of muffin with coffee and bent forward in the chair, her elbows resting just above her knees and her feet a shoulder's width apart. She set her coffee mug on the floor between her feet and looked up warily.

"What do you want to know?"

"We all have a story. We can't run from our past forever. Do you want to tell me what happened to you?"

Mare picked up the coffee mug and walked with it to the kitchen counter. She didn't turn around to face Lou as she began her answer.

"When I was a little kid, I lived on a farm—I guess it was a commune—with a bunch of other families. My dad was like ...

this *leader* ... of everyone there, but he was into some sick religious crap. And he messed with me, you know. He got my mom hooked on drugs, but she managed to get me and her outta there just before my dad brainwashed everyone into this mass suicide. Told 'em they were going to see Jesus or something."

"How old were you?"

"About twelve. And then I was in a foster home. But Uncle Miles—he wasn't my real uncle, you know?—well, he was always on the sauce. And he could get real mean. So I left."

Lou took her time before responding. "Who else knows about this, Mare?"

"No one. You're not gonna turn me in, are you?" Mare turned around from the counter and faced Lou, her right hand involuntarily tightened into a fist at her side.

Lou shook her head. "Now I see where you're going with the graffiti, Mare. It's powerful. Maybe I can help spread your message. I've done magazine work. I think I could get you into *Rolling Stone*."

"No way! That's just for rock stars." She eyed the magazine on the counter and reached for it.

"I've done a few pieces for them. Graffiti is hot in New York. The story of a small-town Georgia girl writing graf to protest the people and institutions who let her down—"

"Wait a minute! If they find out who I am, they can put me away somewhere! I'm only sixteen."

"There are ways to get emancipated early, Mare. I'll help you. I want you to go back to school, to study art. I know some people at SCAD."

"What is SCAD?!"

"Savannah College of Art and Design."

"But I didn't even finish high school ..."

"You can get your GED—it's just a simple test—I know you can pass it."

Mare's head was spinning. *How could this Lou person know I could pass some test? What does she want from me? Why is she being so nice? No one gives you something for nothing.*

"You don't have to decide anything today—oh, look, the light is shifting." Lou got up and moved into the living room and began to make preparations for the day's shoot. "Come on in here, Mare."

She watched Lou drape an entire wall with a black sheet, then place a large piece of plywood in front of the wall.

"Get out a few cans. I want to shoot you writing graf."

Mare brought the paint over to the wall and looked at Lou like she was crazy. "In here? The fumes will be strong. Paint will get on your floors."

Lou laughed. "It's a rented apartment, Mare. I've opened the windows and covered the floor with plastic. It's okay."

Mare let Lou direct her through a series of shots while she threw up her tag, "Cherry Bomb." Zooming in to capture Mare's expressions, Lou again danced gracefully around her subject. But at the end of the day, Mare didn't feel good about the shoot. It didn't feel authentic with Lou staging it inside an apartment.

"Can I stay and see the pictures?"

"Sure, I'll develop the film tonight. Stay for dinner?"

"I guess so." Mare yawned and slumped onto the couch.

"Take a nap while I work on the proofs and start dinner. I'm sure you haven't been getting enough sleep."

Mare leaned back into the cushions. She was asleep in two minutes and awoke to unfamiliar aromas coming from the kitchen. She found Lou stirring a pot of soup and putting out slices of round, flat bread. And a brownish-looking dip.

"What's that stuff?"

"Oh, it's Baba Ghanoush—eggplant dip. You eat it with pita bread. The soup is lentil. My mother was a vegetarian, so I guess that's another thing in my genes."

Mare watched Lou scoop up the dip with a triangle of the pita bread and followed her lead. She liked the soup better, and raised the bowl to drink the last sip.

"Have you finished with the pictures?"

"Yes. Would you like to see them? They're dry now."

Lou went into the darkroom and returned with a stack of prints. They looked at them together in silence for a few minutes. Then Mare said, "Something's not right. It's just not the same, doing graf on a piece of plywood in an apartment. It's not ... it's not real, you know?"

"I completely agree, Mare, and I want to ask you something. What would you say to my coming with you on your next throwup?"

"I don't know. I usually work in the dark, just before dawn. You'd have to use a flash. We'd get caught for sure."

"I've done work with low light. I'd really like to try."

"Okay, then. I'm about ready to hit up my biggest target—the Catholic Church over on Hazel Street. It's nearby. Those side streets will make for an easy escape."

"So, what's the real target?"

"I just told you—"

Mare got up and paced the room. Her hazel eyes darkened and her hands formed fists at her sides. "I guess it's God—if he even exists. And my father."

"What about Uncle Miles?"

"Him too."

Lou crossed the room and hugged Mare tenderly. Mare let go of feelings she had been holding back for years. Soon Lou was stroking Mare's hair and wiping away her tears. She was, Mare realized, the first person that had ever shown her kindness.

"Don't leave," Lou said softly. "You don't have to sleep on the streets. You can stay here, with me."

. . .

Over the next few days, they settled into an easy rhythm of sharing meals and stories. Mare showed Lou more of her piece-book, and Lou showed Mare some of her work in *Rolling Stone* and other magazines. Mare gradually began to trust Lou. One day she asked, "Would you ever photograph me nude, the way you've done some of those other people?"

Lou looked surprised at the question. "Would you want me to?"

"I don't know. Maybe."

"I try to photograph each person in a way that tells their story. That reveals their soul. You're too young."

Lou's protectiveness increased Mare's confidence in their plan to share her next project. The next afternoon they walked the few blocks from Lou's apartment to the church, arriving at dusk. No cars were in the parking lot or on the street. Mare went to work quickly, setting cans while Lou readied her camera. Mare looked at Lou. It felt different, more exciting, when someone was watching. They exchanged a smile.

Mare began with a woman holding a child on her lap—like a Madonna—with the young girl from her other pieces clinging to the woman. The figures were both mouthless. Fear emanated from their faces. This time, the large shadow of the man towering over them had a beard. He wore a robe with a cross on the front of it. The man reached toward the woman and children with a knife in his hand. (She couldn't bring herself to paint his penis.) It was a powerful image. Mare was almost too overcome with anger and grief to add her tag when it was finished.

Lou captured the scene using a flash for the final shots. Mare put the cans into her backpack and was ready to hurry away when they heard a car door slam. Before they could make a run for it, a young woman called out and hurried toward them.

"Wait! Please!"

Mare knew it was too late to run. And it wasn't the police. So what was the worst that could happen? As the woman approached in the falling darkness, Mare spotted a camera and notepad and knew Lou saw it, too. It hit them both just before she introduced herself.

"I'm Margaret Adams. From *The Macon News*."

FOUR

LOU SPOKE FIRST. "How did you know where to come?"

"I've been driving around every night within a few blocks of the first painting, hoping to find the artist." Margaret looked up at the graffiti on the church wall, and then at Mare, still hiding under her hoodie. "I guess I found him."

Mare pulled the hoodie back and looked at her.

"But ... you're a girl."

Lou stepped forward and extended her hand. "This is Mare. I'm Lou."

Margaret noticed Lou's camera case. "Who hired you?"

Lou paused, considering her answer. "I freelance."

"Wait—Lou? Lou Lieberman? *The* Lou Lieberman?"

Lou put her hands in her pockets and nodded.

"What are you doing in Macon?"

"I'm here on assignment. And then I met Mare and we've been collaborating on a couple of projects."

"Really?" Turning to Mare, Margaret asked, "Would you mind if I photographed you with your graffiti for *The News*?"

"No way!" Mare looked at Lou, then back at Margaret. "You trying to get me arrested?" She pulled her hoodie back over her head and crossed her arms over her chest.

"How old are you, Mare?" Margaret wrote without looking at her notepad.

"I'm sixteen—almost seventeen."

"I could speak with Father Joseph, tell him you're a minor. He wouldn't press charges. He might want to talk with you, though."

"Father Joseph? He's some kind of priest or something, right?"

"Well, yes, he's the pastor of this church."

"I'm not talking to no priest."

"Let's take one thing at a time," Lou said. "We'd prefer that you only photograph her work, and leave Mare out of the shot."

"You have an exclusive deal with her, Ms. Lieberman?"

"We haven't signed a contract, but I think this is what she wants." She looked at Mare, who nodded her agreement.

"May I ask you a few questions, then?"

Margaret Adams struck Mare as a bit too eager. But Lou seemed to approve of this, too, so Mare nodded.

"Take your pictures first, and then we'll go back to my apartment for the interview."

"Would you mind? That would be great."

Mare and Lou watched Margaret photograph the piece. The emotional impact of the work began to hit Mare as the lights in the parking lot came on, throwing an eerie blue-gray film across the wall of graffiti. The voices of Lou and Margaret faded into the background as Mare stood, trance-like, absorbing the moment.

"You might want to use a filter," Lou suggested.

Margaret reached into her pouch and attached a glass filter to the outside of her lens and took several more shots. Afterward, they all got into the reporter's car and headed to Lou's apartment. Mare and Margaret followed Lou inside and, exhausted from the day's adventures—Mare's graffiti hit, Lou's photo shoot, and Margaret's discovery as she followed her reporter's nose to the church at dusk—they collapsed into the chairs in the kitchen and waited for the coffee to finish percolating.

"I hadn't planned on guests for supper." Lou opened the refrigerator and pulled out a loaf of bread. "Anyone want a sandwich?"

"Sure. I'm famished," Margaret said. Then, her excitement clearly building, she added, "It's not every day I have supper with a graffiti artist and a photographer for *Rolling Stone!*"

Mare yawned and shook her head yes. She looked at Margaret, anxious about the interview. Lou poured three mugs of coffee and pulled some tuna and lettuce from the fridge. She reached into the cabinet and found some peanut butter and brought it with her to the table.

"Y'all ready to get started?"

For the next few minutes Mare recounted her story while Margaret took notes. She left out some of the more graphic details.

"So, you ran away from a cult and then a foster home, and started throwing up graffiti?" Margaret looked at Mare, and then at Lou, her eyebrows forming a question mark. "There's got to be more to the story than that."

"It's like I told Lou—I got beat up some and stuff. It's no big deal."

Lou went back to the fridge for jelly for Mare's sandwich.

Bringing it back to the table, she stood beside Mare and placed her hand on her shoulder. "I think that's enough for now, don't you, Margaret?"

"Sure. Let's go talk with Father Joseph before I submit the story to my editor." Margaret looked at her watch. "Actually, it's too late tonight. Mind if I use your phone, Lou?"

Lou pointed to the wall phone by the refrigerator. Margaret checked her notebook for the number and dialed.

"Father Joseph? Margaret Adams at the *News*. Yes, sir, Nancy Sue's daughter. No, sir, they don't call me Maggie anymore." Margaret paused. "Oh, you've seen it already. That's actually why I'm calling. I'm here with the—the artist. We'd like to come over to talk with you." Another pause. "Tomorrow morning? Could you? Great. We'll see you around nine."

"Did he sound angry?" Mare's voice cracked. The thought of meeting with a priest struck more fear in her than throwing up graffiti on the side of his church. "What did he say?"

"Something like, 'the darnedest thing happened over here at the church tonight.'" Margaret smiled at Mare. "We can all go in my car. I'll pick you up around eight forty-five."

• • •

They made the short drive the next morning over to Saint Joseph's in silence. As they approached the parking lot, all three pairs of eyes were glued to Mare's piece. It looked larger in the mid-morning light, more powerful somehow. Margaret parked near the door to the building. Mare took a deep breath as Margaret opened the door and led them down the hall to Father Joseph's office. He was waiting for them.

"Well, hello, Margaret."

"Father Joseph." She bowed slightly.

"And who are your friends?"

"This is Lou—Anne Louise—Lieberman."

"The photographer?"

"You know my work?" Lou asked, sounding shocked.

Father Joseph smiled. "I'm a priest, not a monk." Turning to Mare, he added, "And you must be—"

"Mare." She cleared her throat several times and stared at the floor.

"I thought I was going to be meeting 'Cherry Bomb' this morning," Father Joseph chuckled.

Mare shrugged.

"Where are my manners? Please have a seat, ladies." Father Joseph indicated a sitting area at one end of the room. Upholstered leather chairs framed an oriental rug. An antique table anchored the sitting area. A bronze lamp shot rays of yellow onto the floor-to-ceiling bookshelves.

"I've seen the pictures you've taken of this young woman's activities in our quiet little town, Margaret. I've been trying to read between the lines, interpret the message behind those dark images." Turning to Mare, he asked, "Would you like to tell me about it, young lady?"

Something about Father Joseph's voice unnerved Mare. She had never met a real priest, although her father and the other leaders at the farm called themselves priests. Was this man really any different? Her voice broke several times and her hands shook as she gave an even more bare-bones version of her story than what she'd told Margaret last night.

Father Joseph listened patiently. Finally he asked, "So, why did you choose our church as the target for this final piece? Have we also hurt you?"

"No ... I mean, I don't know you. But what makes you any different from my father, or Uncle Miles?"

"Your foster father?"

"Yeah, that piece of shit."

"And so you hold all men responsible. And you had no place

to tell your story. So that's why the figures in your paintings—the young girls—don't have mouths."

Mare was determined not to cry and met Father Joseph's words with an unflinching stare.

"You're not going to press charges, are you, Father?" Margaret asked.

"No, of course not. But there will be consequences."

Here it comes. Mare looked at the floor again while Father Joseph talked.

"Someone is going to have to paint over the graffiti—we can't leave it on the church building. You understand that, don't you, Mare?"

"I guess so."

"I was thinking it would be nice to have a sort of mural on that side of the building. Where you painted your graffiti piece. Something that could tell a more redemptive story than the one you've given voice to. If I can find an artist to take on the project, would you be willing to serve as his assistant?"

Mare froze. She stared for a moment, wide-eyed and open-mouthed. "I've never done anything but graf. I wouldn't know how to help."

"Well, you could do the preparations for the mural—painting over your graffiti before the artist arrives on site. I'm in no hurry. Maybe your message needs a little time to sink into the hearts and minds of the town, to prompt them to protect our women and children from abuse."

Mare could hardly believe Father Joseph. A man of the cloth being kind to her, wanting to help her. There must be more to it than this.

"I'd love to stay in town during the project," Lou offered, "and photograph the mural as it goes up. Would that be a problem, Father?"

The priest smiled. "*Rolling Stone's* readers won't know what hit them, now will they?"

"And may I cover the story for the *News*?" Margaret was already making notes without waiting for an answer.

"I guess all that's left to do is contact the artist. Oh, and where are you staying, Mare?"

Mare looked at Lou.

"She's staying with me," Lou said, "at least for as long as I'm in town."

"You know we have to get in touch with the social services folks. Let them know where you are."

"They won't make me go back, will they? I can't do that—I *won't*. I'll run away again, I swear!" Mare started for the door. Father Joseph raised his hands, palms up. He stepped close to Mare and motioned for her to stay, guiding her to a chair near his desk.

"No, no. Calm down now. No one is sending you back there. But your foster parents may be prosecuted. We'll see what the authorities decide to do."

"I have an idea." Lou looked at Father Joseph, then at Mare. "I went to school at SCAD. I think I could get you a scholarship to study art there, if you're willing to put in the work to get your GED first."

"There are people here in the parish who could help with that," Father Joseph added. "I know a retired schoolteacher who could tutor you for the test. Let me make a few phone calls. Say, are you girls hungry? I think there's some cereal or maybe some biscuits in the kitchen."

They followed Father Joseph down the hall toward the church kitchen. Mare paused at the entrance of the sanctuary, which smelled of incense and beeswax. She had never been inside a Catholic church before and found the images and smells intriguing.

"Would you like to go inside?" Father Joseph asked.

"I don't care. I just noticed the smell."

Father Joseph laughed and led the way. Mare watched as Father Joseph and then Margaret stopped in front of the altar, knelt, and crossed themselves before taking a seat on one of the pews. Mare ran her hands over the arm of a wooden pew, smooth with the patina of its years. As she slid in beside the others, her eyes continued to take in the glimmer of candlelight on the brass candelabras. Only the sun's rays—refracted through stained-glass windows—lit the church, even in late morning. And although it felt a little creepy being in there, Mare couldn't help but admire the paintings. Father Joseph noticed her staring at them.

"Most of the paintings in here are Western religious paintings, typical of Catholic churches, as are the stained-glass windows. But over here," he said, pointing to an area on the side of the aisle, "we have a Byzantine icon, which you see more often in Eastern Orthodox Churches."

The women turned to look at the icon, and then got up and walked closer, following Father Joseph's lead. The icon was sitting on a wooden stand. A brass container beside it held several partially-burned candles. Margaret asked questions, but her voice faded into the background as Mare found herself enraptured by the painting. It was of a woman—possibly an older woman because her hair looked gray, almost white. She wore only a cloak which covered about half of her torso, leaving the other half naked. Her flesh was not painted realistically, with full bosoms and a woman's natural shapeliness. Instead it was very primitive, almost cartoonish, with exaggerated lines indicating her rib cage, and unnaturally elongated features.

Little inverted triangles were painted under her eyes, giving the appearance of a mime's sad expression. Her mouth was very small, her hair unkempt. She looked wild, but she held a cross in her right hand. The background of the painting showed a desert-like terrain, mostly sand and rocks. Mare could feel the woman looking back at her—*through* her—to her soul.

"Who ... who is she?" Mare asked.

"This is Saint Mary of Egypt," the priest replied. "A prostitute in fourth-century Egypt who repented and became a desert dweller and miracle-worker."

"So, how did you come to have this painting, Father?" Margaret was writing in her notebook again.

"An elderly Coptic woman who lived in our community brought it to the church a number of years ago. The icon had been in her family for several generations. And since there was no Orthodox Church in Macon, she brought it here and asked me to place it where it would be treated with proper respect."

"What's 'Coptic'?" Margaret asked.

"The Copts are Egyptian Christians. They have a special devotion to Saint Mary of Egypt."

"Is she still alive—that woman—the one who had the icon?" Mare asked.

"She passed on about four years ago, I guess."

"Right about the time my mother left me." What she didn't say was that the woman in the painting bore an eerie resemblance to her mother.

"Where is your mother now, Mare?" Father Joseph asked.

Now Mare was sorry she had mentioned her mother. Talking about her stirred up feelings she would rather not feel. "I don't know. She said she'd come back for me when she got clean and sober. But I never heard from her again."

"Have you tried to find her?"

"Hell, no!" Mare paused. "I was afraid of being put back in the system if I started asking around. She's probably strung out on drugs somewhere, maybe even dead. Who cares?"

The four of them stood silently, looking at the icon. Mare glanced over at Father Joseph. His lips were moving and at one point he closed his eyes, made the sign of the cross, and leaned forward to kiss the icon, right on the saint's hand—the one holding the cross. As he and the others began to leave, Mare stayed behind with her memories. A minute later Lou stuck her head back into the sanctuary.

"Mare? Are you coming? Father Joseph has some food ready for us in the kitchen."

• • •

Mare spent the next few weeks studying for her GED and living with Lou in her studio apartment. Looking up from one of the study guide worksheets one morning, she screamed, "I hate math! Why does someone who just wants to be an artist need to know this crap?"

Lou laughed as she followed Mare's voice into the kitchen. "I'm afraid I can't help you there. I guess our brains work the same way." She gave Mare a hug before sitting down at the table with her.

"I'm sorry to complain." Mare put down her pencil and looked into Lou's face. "You've been so great to me—everyone here has. But sometimes ..."

"Sometimes what?"

"Well, sometimes I get scared. I mean, is *Rolling Stone* really paying you for all this time you're spending with me? And the scholarship at SCAD—is that really going to happen?"

"Hey, I promise you *Stone* is happy with the samples I've sent them so far. This is going to be a top-drawer piece. And everything is going to work out at SCAD. You need to quit worrying and concentrate on passing that GED."

Mare smiled weakly and picked her pencil back up. But as she tried to return to the fractions on the page, her mind went elsewhere. Being with Lou—who felt something like a big sister—made her think more about her mother. And her brothers. And as messed up as it was, she missed the community she had as a child back at Heaven's Gate.

So when Father Joseph hired an artist to paint a mural over Mare's graffiti piece at the church, Mare was a bit excited to help—to be part of a project with someone else. The artist was a fine arts major at Mercer. At first she worried that he might be condescending since she was just a street artist. But he treated her with respect, involving her in the design process as well as the actual painting. Working with him made her wonder what Phoenix and Jagger might be doing if they were still alive. But she couldn't dwell on the past—there was work to be done. Standing on the scaffolding with him alongside the church building as Margaret and Lou documented their work, Mare honestly felt like she was part of something that mattered. And when he showed her the iconographic figure of Saint Joseph he planned to use as the centerpiece for the mural, she asked who it was.

"Saint Joseph is the patron saint of families, since he was the Father in the Holy Family, and he took care of Mary and Jesus," the artist explained. "I wanted to show him taking care of women and children today."

The painting showed women and children in modern-day clothing, gathered around Saint Joseph. Mare felt a strange mixture of hope and sorrow.

"Are you enjoying working on the mural?" Margaret asked one day when the project was near completion. She and Mare were sitting under a tree near the parking lot of the church, enjoying an unusual late-summer breeze as Mare took a break from the work. The artist was putting finishing touches on parts of the scene and Lou was taking pictures.

"It's okay. Not like writing graf, though."

"What do you mean?"

"I guess I miss the excitement."

Margaret stopped writing. Lou finished taking pictures and headed to her car. "You coming, Mare?"

"That's okay. I think I'll walk."

On her way to Lou's apartment, Mare passed by several abandoned buildings, their blank walls beckoning her like dope to an addict. She had only two cans in her backpack. And she hadn't worked out any new pieces since she started helping with the mural at the church. If she left her tag, everyone would know it was her because of Margaret's newspaper articles.

Should I quit writing graf altogether? Get a new tag?

. . .

A couple of days after the mural was finished, Father Joseph called Mare at Lou's apartment and asked her to meet with him in his office. Lou was on a shoot and said she would join them later.

Mare entered the priest's office with a lighter spirit than she'd had at the beginning of summer and stopped in front of his desk. "What's up?"

"SCAD has offered you a scholarship." Father Joseph came around his desk and stood two feet from her. "They just sent me a recommendation form to sign."

"Really?!? You mean ... I'm *in*?"

Lou came rushing into the room. Father Joseph smiled at her. "Hello, Lou. Please join us. I was just telling Mare the good news. SCAD has offered her a scholarship."

"I know! The dean called right after Mare left to come over here. Looks like you've got a place in the freshman class this fall!"

Mare looked at Lou for a moment, then at Father Joseph. Then she sank into the chair next to the one Lou was taking. "Where will I live?" she asked quietly.

"In one of the dorms or maybe a student apartment in

Savannah," Lou said. "It's all worked out. You'll need a part-time job, but the school can help you with that."

"The whole community is behind you," Father Joseph added.

"And you're in for a special treat," Lou said. "Elaine de Kooning will be a visiting professor for the next two years. Contract's signed and everything."

"Who's she?"

"One of New York's top female Ab Ex painters."

"Ab Ex?"

"Abstract Expressionism. Right up your alley. Maybe she'll keep you off the street."

Not likely. But Mare had to admit that all of this sounded positive.

• • •

Father Joseph and the good people of his parish came through for Mare in ways she couldn't have dreamed of. They even gave her a bicycle so she could get around town more easily.

Leaving Macon was surprisingly difficult. Mare had memories of leaving two other places in her young life—Heaven's Gate and Uncle Miles' house in Forsyth—but those were escapes, places she was running from. Macon was the first place she ever felt safe, and she spent her last few days riding her bike around to all the places she had thrown up graffiti. Some had been painted over, but others remained. She stopped by The Bean to say goodbye to the older waitress who had treated her so kindly.

"Are you done with school?" she asked. Mare kept her smile to herself. The waitress, apparently, still thought Mare was a student at Mercer.

"No. I'm actually going to study art at SCAD. Over in Savannah."

"That's wonderful, honey. We'll miss you here." She made Mare her favorite drink, a latte with cinnamon on top. "On me."

The toughest goodbye was Lou. Margaret and Father Joseph joined them for supper at the apartment on her last night in town—she would board a bus for Savannah in the morning.

"You're going to do great at school," Lou said as Father Joseph and Margaret were leaving. "We'll be checking up on you, you know."

"I'm going to miss seeing your work around town," Margaret added with a smile.

Father Joseph gave her a light hug. "Come back and visit when you can."

Mare said little, not trusting herself to hold it together if she tried to express how she felt toward them. They were the first friends she'd ever had. But what really brought tears to Mare's eyes was when Lou made sure she was tucked in before going to bed—she gave Mare a tender little kiss on her forehead. Like a mother would have, Mare knew.

She couldn't get any words out, but she took Lou's hand and squeezed.

FIVE

ELAINE WONDERED HOW she had ended up here. In this southern coastal city, teaching neophytes the art she had spent a lifetime learning and polishing. She had sacrificed more personal freedom and integrity than these children could ever know. When the college invited her for a two-year stint as visiting professor, she was at a low point—vulnerable, needing the money and, perhaps more significantly, the power and the independence. Her place as a female artist in the male-dominated world of abstract expressionism needed to be acknowledged. Her husband had reluctantly supported her decision to accept the position, though not really understanding her need for approval and artistic intimacy.

"Isn't it enough to be my wife, my protégé?" Willem had said after returning from another jaunt at an artists' colony, where he wooed the young students and fed his ego on their accolades. The discussion was just before Elaine's move south. "When are you going to stay home with me, for good?"

"You don't need me in your harem, Bill. I am needed elsewhere. Eager young minds about to ruin a lot of canvases. Without my help."

It had been difficult enough to put up with his casual affairs through the years, but when he and Joan Ward—that tart from the Village he carried on with during one of their separations—had a love child, she thought that was the final straw. Bill and Joan even shared a house in East Hampton for a while in the '60s. Why did she keep taking him back? Her bond with this brilliant man who seemed to toss her aside as easily as one of his practice canvases was impossible to sever permanently. But she had to get away from time to time.

And so she left him in New York and moved to Savannah for two years, to a backhouse belonging to one of the city's old-money families. She was only a visitor—albeit an honored one—to the school, to the city, to the South.

She called out her students' names, these kids who were mostly eighteen to twenty-something years old. Her younger self was reflected back to her as she tried to read the stories behind the faces that eagerly awaited her instruction and hungered for her approval. She craved their attention just as much as they needed her—the artist, the teacher. At age sixty-five, she would not let them see her own hunger. She would present herself always as a sophisticated traveler from the big city to their little southern world, bearing keys to unlock their provincial minds, new colors for their small-town palettes, new ways of seeing, new tools to capture life as images on paper and canvas. She felt a kind of emotional tug-of-war with them as she worked to establish her power over each student.

"Stephen Alexander."

"Here."

Stephen was a graphic design major, his white dress shirt with sleeves rolled up, unbuttoned at the collar, skinny black tie loosened, the knot sitting casually just below his Adam's apple. She could meet his eyes and gain ground.

"Where are you from, Mr. Alexander?"

"Baton Rouge, Louisiana, ma'am."

"It says here that you are a graphic design major. Hoping to make money in advertising instead of learning the skills of fine art?"

"No, ma'am. I mean, I'm not sure what I want to do."

"As I thought."

Elaine felt a rush as she continued the game, engaging each of the male students, watching them lose their footing, unable to hold their own against her.

She faltered when she faced off with the young women. It was not their appearance that threatened her—years of yoga and a strict vegetarian diet had kept her body slim and youthful. Sure, years of alcohol and cigarettes had taken their toll on her skin, and a nagging cough occasionally reminded her of her mortality, but she knew she was still a classy woman. Her sense of style was evident in her blunt-cut, chin-length hair and geometric bangs, her pencil-leg slacks, over-sized blue shirt and ballet flats. Very much like the version of herself that hung in the National Gallery in Washington, D.C. Her looks belied her age and she used them, with an added measure of sophistication, to intimidate or to attract, to fit the need of the moment.

Which face, then, would she show the young women in her class on this first day? Would any of them be able to penetrate her fortress the way all those women in New York had paraded themselves through her marriage over the past thirty years? But this was a new place, a new time. She would reclaim herself during her stay here.

"Mary Katherine Henry."

A girl pulled the crumpled class schedule from her mouth as she stumbled in the door just in time to answer, "Here! But it's Mare."

Elaine looked down at her list of students briefly, then back up at Mare, who was fumbling with her portfolio and supplies. Their eyes met.

"But Mary Katherine is fine, ma'am."

Elaine had known about Mare's scholarship before arriving in Savannah. She had seen the pictures in *Rolling Stone*. She was curious about this young woman, the dark stories behind her art, and whether or not Mare had anything else to offer the art world. Would her talent hold up outside the realm of bubble letters and spray paint? Most of the New York graf writers did not move beyond the primitive images they threw up on subway walls. Only a few made a name for themselves and displayed in the galleries.

Something familiar about Mare's face caught Elaine off guard. Was that admiration she saw in her expression, or was it a ploy? What did this girl really think of her? The others were less formidable. Flannery MacGrath smiled through her armor: those chains would have to go. Kimberly Pittman, clearly old-money Atlanta, probably fell in love with the *idea* of being an artist. But could she draw? Could she see beyond the surface of the world's shell?

"You might want to leave the pearls behind, Miss Pittman. We'll be working with a lot of messy materials in here."

The girl blushed. Elaine kept her smile to herself.

Refreshing. You don't see that much any more.

The room held its breath. But there were no more victims of

Elaine de Kooning's sharp edge that day. She had established herself, her place in the classroom. She lit a cigarette and delivered her introductory remarks as she described the upcoming projects in her studio class.

SIX

THE CLASSROOM WAS housed in one of the original buildings belonging to Savannah College of Art and Design, which was only in its fifth year of existence. Yesterday Mare had ridden her bicycle through the tree-lined cobblestone streets. In the city's two hundred and fiftieth year, with its moss-covered oaks, ante-bellum homes and churches, and park-like city squares—she was preparing to rewrite her own history. Well, if only it were that simple. The admissions counselor told Mare that her life was now a blank canvas waiting for her teachers to breathe life onto it.

In the studio, the other students stared at her. They had to know who she was, Mare figured. Her story was all over the media with headlines like MIDNIGHT GRAFFITI ARTIST STRIKES AGAIN and ANOTHER CHERRY BOMB FOUND ON WASHINGTON AVENUE. Oh, and her personal favorite, MONROE COUNTY ORPHAN WINS SCHOLARSHIP TO SCAD. Monroe County *orphan*. The reporter probably didn't mean to be unkind; she was just stating what she understood to be the facts. At least she didn't say *whore*, which is how Mare saw herself when she peered into the rearview mirror at that backwoods town with its lonely dirt roads and isolated dwellings, well out of view of the good people of Forsyth, Georgia.

A dozen pairs of eyes watched her search the classroom for a place on the back row where she could hide from their stares. The upstairs room was brightly lit by the morning sun, which poured in through the windows and danced through the leaves of the tall oak tree that brushed against the brick wall. A slight muskiness mixed with the smell of pigments left over from last semester's classes.

She found her way in her faded jeans and white tank top, her steely green eyes and heavy black eye makeup masking the frightened little girl inside, a row of earrings along the rim of her left ear peeking through her short, streaked, black-and-blond hair. Her canvas high tops squeaked on the linoleum floor; her dog tags clinked together as she walked toward an empty desk. A Goth-looking girl in a micro miniskirt and Doc Martens offered a half-smile from the desk to Mare's left and whispered, "Hi. I'm Flannery."

"Hi," she whispered back, not making eye contact as she took a seat. To her right, a longhaired boy was really looking her up and down. Mare tried to focus on the printed materials on his desk. *Where'd he get those? Does everyone have them? Am I already in trouble because I was late?* She answered the boy's stare with raised eyebrows, noticing that his fingers were smudged with charcoal, a mark of their trade. He turned then to face the instructor, who had just began to read from a syllabus, and Mare did, too, at the sound of the woman's voice—its tone at once rich and confident. As Lou had promised, it was Elaine de Kooning, one of a small number of female artists who were part of the elite New York School of abstract expressionism that started in the 1940s and '50s. Mare could hardly believe she was in the same room with her.

She imagined Elaine working in the salons in New York, pursued by students and art enthusiasts. Lou explained that she'd been mentored by her husband, Willem de Kooning; Mare, of course, had worked beside her mother and brothers on the farm. Could their lives have somehow intersected in this magical world where art was not something to be ashamed of? It didn't seem remotely possible.

Yet there was something eerily familiar about Professor de Kooning.

• • •

A few days later, as the students were emulating the grattage technique of the surrealists—scraping dry paint off their canvases with trowels—Elaine approached Mare, who was working in tempera instead.

"Didn't you hear my lecture on Miró and Ernst?"

Oh, shit, I'm already in trouble. At first Mare didn't look up from her painting. After a few brush strokes, she nodded, took a deep breath, and sat back in her chair. "I like their work okay—especially Miró—but I don't like painting with a palette knife. I like brushes."

"Miró didn't limit himself to knives, Mare."

"Yeah, I know. That tapestry thing he did, the one up in New York City?" She put down her brush and looked up at Elaine. "Have you seen it? In person, I mean?"

"Yes, it's magnificent. It's at the World Trade Center. But

quit trying to change the subject." Elaine walked around behind Mare to view her work. "Your first pieces were done with a can of spray paint. Now you chose sable brushes and tempera?"

"I used tempera when I was a kid, before I did graf. Still like it sometimes."

Mare watched Elaine inspect the piece on her desk. Abstract images repeated across the canvas from left to right. Each successive figure was smaller than the last, and partly hidden from view by a larger image in front—as if mirrors were set across from one another. The image seemed to gradually disappear.

"Good use of perspective, Mare." Elaine pointed to the largest figure. "If you want the figure to disappear, use less viscosity with each subsequent image."

"I tried that already. The paint gets too watery."

"Try binding it with egg emulsion. Iconographers have used egg tempera for centuries."

"Yeah, I saw an icon once. At a church in Macon. It was really old but the colors were good. Does the egg yolk also make them last?"

"Right. It binds the pigments. Did you like the icon?"

Mare put her brush down and leaned against her desk on one elbow, her hand under her chin. She looked up at Elaine and answered, "Well, I'm not into religion or anything, but there was something ... I don't know what. Something about that picture kinda grabbed me."

"Was it Byzantine or Russian? What style?"

"Father Joseph—the priest at the church—said it was Coptic, whatever that means."

"Oh, really? No wonder you liked it. Coptic images are stark, primitive, like abstractions of Western religious art. Icons have something in common with graffiti, you know."

You might be a big-shot artist and all, but you don't know shit about graffiti. "Actually, no," Mare said, leaning back in her chair and crossing her arms. "Graf isn't about religion."

Elaine reached for a nearby chair, pulled it beside Mare's desk, and sat down. "Maybe not, but you know how graffiti artists are called graf *writers*? Well, iconographers *write* icons. But they use paint, just like you do with graffiti."

"They got a story to tell, like graf writers?"

"They definitely have a story to tell. When a writer tells the life of a saint, it's called *hagiography*. When it's told with paint, it's called *iconography*. Would you like to see some books with illustrations of icons?"

"I guess ..."

"Come by my office after class."

Elaine got up and moved on to critique other students' work, leaving Mare staring off into space and lost in thought. She was talking with Elaine de Kooning about pictures she saw *in a church*, and now the oh-so-important visiting professor wanted Mare to come to her office? She wasn't sure how she felt about all of this—it was happening awfully fast.

Flannery, working nearby, shot Mare a smirky look. "Getting chummy with de Kooning, huh? What's that about?"

"Nothing. Jeez, she's just trying to help."

Flannery returned to her work, but her question distracted Mare from her painting. She cleaned up her space and headed to Elaine's office before studio was over.

• • •

Elaine de Kooning's office turned out to be a shrine to her Ab Ex roots. Her work was mythological, primitive. In a picture of her at a gallery show in New York, she stood beside a mixed-media work in oil and old newspaper. *Winter Landscape Collage* evoked a wintry scene with gestural evergreen brushstrokes over a field of white. Another photograph showed her with an ink and gouache portrait of a woman in a pensive pose, hands together in her lap, her expression dark and empty.

"One of the first pieces I sold," Elaine said as she came into her office, startling Mare.

"Oh, sorry—I didn't mean—is it okay I'm looking at these?"

Elaine laughed. "Of course. That's why they're on the wall. The ones I don't want anyone to see are hidden in drawers or behind cabinet doors."

"That one is beautiful." Mare pointed to the landscape collage. "But I like this one better." She was standing in front of the portrait of the woman.

"*Beautiful*? That's a term rarely applied to painting any more." Elaine sat down at her desk and pointed at a nearby chair. Mare dropped her backpack on the floor and sat. Elaine lit a cigarette and looked over her shoulder at the pictures on the wall. "These days, struggling with one's demons produces art that's harsh, and sometimes ugly."

"Like my graf?"

"Yes. Those images weren't borne of blithe happiness and childhood pleasures, were they? Art proceeds from life—even at your young age—and the sometimes painful things you've lived."

She pulled on her cigarette as their eyes met and held for the moment. Mare looked away and shifted in her chair to deflect Elaine's comment. "So, where are those icons you wanted to show me?"

Elaine stubbed out her cigarette in a brown glass ashtray, got up, and pulled a book from the cluttered shelves behind her desk. She sat in a chair next to Mare and opened the book. The first pages she flipped through were mostly traditional religious paintings—the kind Mare supposed one might see in Catholic churches and art museums. But then Elaine turned to a primitive painting of a Madonna and child, their proportions skewed (large eyes, elongated features, small mouths) with simple, dark outlines and uncomplicated highlights. "Here they are. The Coptic icons."

"Yeah, these look kind of like the one I saw at the church." Mare turned the pages, looking at the icons quizzically. "Almost like cartoons, like kids' pictures."

"Yes. They're not meant to be realistic."

"How do you know about this stuff?"

"I traveled to Egypt," Elaine said. "Toured Coptic churches, mainly to see the art. It struck me how abstract these icons are, as opposed to Western religious pictures."

"And how did they get the paint to look like that—the way it's thick in some areas but more transparent in others? Is this tempera?"

"They used egg emulsion—you separate the egg white from the yolk, and then carefully remove the membrane before mixing the yolk with the dry pigments. The egg acts as a binder, so the paintings last for centuries. But it also makes the paint easier to work with in varying opacities—like when you were wanting to fade your colors without getting too watery."

"Cool."

They turned the pages of the book together, Mare's hand occasionally brushing against Elaine's. She felt something strong in the contact—intimate but not sexual. She wondered if Elaine felt it, too, as a nervous laugh got caught in her throat. Then Elaine sat up straighter and faced her.

"Mare, would you like to see more egg tempera icons, in person?"

"Where?"

"There's a Coptic church in Atlanta. I was planning on going there next weekend for an art show. We could make it a field trip."

"You mean for the class?"

"No. Just us."

Wow. "Where would we stay? I don't have money for a hotel or anything."

"I've already booked a room. You can stay with me."

"Well ... I'm supposed to work in the print room Saturday. It's part of my scholarship package, making sure there's ink in the machines and fun stuff like that."

"I'll talk with your supervisor. You can work a double on another weekend." Elaine lit another cigarette and leaned back in her chair. "What do you think?"

"I'd love to. Thanks."

Mare stood, picked up her backpack, and started for the door. As she made her way down the hall, the prospect of spending that much time alone with her professor made her nervous for reasons she couldn't put her finger on.

But she knew she wanted to explore them.

PART TWO

SEVEN

ELAINE AND MARE hit the road for Atlanta on Friday afternoon and went straight to the gallery opening in Buckhead. Elaine explained that she had promised her friend Felix de Weldon that she'd be there for his show; he was big in the avant-garde scene in New York and had brought his work to the South.

"Elaine! You came!" Felix approached them with outstretched arms and hugged Elaine warmly. Then he saw Mare. "And who is this scrumptious creature?"

"This is Mare, one of my students at SCAD. Mare, this is Felix de Weldon."

Mare knew to be polite and gripped Felix's hand awkwardly. It was still uncomfortable to shake the hand of a man after what she'd been through.

"Mare got her start as a graf writer."

"Graf writer? A *girl*? In the *South*?"

"She was throwing her stuff up in Macon. Lou Lieberman discovered her."

"You know, I think I saw that in *Rolling Stone*. You're Cherry Bomb?"

He knows who I am? "Uh ... that's my tag."

A white-aproned waiter carrying trays of champagne approached.

"Lovely." Felix took two flutes and offered them to Elaine and Mare. Mare wasn't sure what to do—she was still very resistant to alcohol after seeing what a monster Uncle Miles became after a few belts, and it didn't matter how cool the SCAD students or anyone else thought they were when bragging about the partying they did.

"You, uh, got any soft drinks?"

"What was I thinking? Ginger ale?" Felix said to the waiter, and kept one of the flutes for himself. Mare sized up the other patrons as the waiter scurried away. The gallery was like a fashion show runway, each wing elbow-to-elbow with filthy-rich types in clothes that probably cost a fortune. She felt self-conscious in her black jeans and t-shirt, which featured an image from Iron Maiden's latest album, "The Number of the Beast."

"Love your shirt," Felix said to Mare with a wink. "So tell me, *Cherry Bomb*, what do you think of the show so far?"

"Uh, well, we just got here. Haven't seen much yet." Mare looked at Elaine for help. "I like the building ... the exposed brick and all that ... must be historic or something, right?"

"Yes, yes!" Felix waved his arms in the air as he spoke. "We just *love* Buckhead Village."

The waiter returned with Mare's ginger ale in a highball glass with ice.

"Cheers!" Felix and Elaine raised their flutes.

Mare took a gulp. She tried to think of something to say that didn't sound stupid. She was also aware that people, here and there, were staring—or at least checking her out. "How do you two know each other?"

"Elaine and I go way back." He chuckled. "We both did Kennedy."

"What he meant was, I painted the president's portrait and he did a bronze of his head," Elaine added quickly.

"You painted Kennedy's portrait. *President* Kennedy?" Mare's mouth fell open as she made no effort to hide her surprise—her awe.

Elaine nodded and took another drink of champagne.

"You know, Mare," Felix said, "Elaine was one of only a few female artists experiencing success in the 1950s and '60s salon scene in New York."

"Maybe so, Felix, but unlike most of our group, I dared to venture outside the boundaries of abstract art. I padded my meager income with portrait commissions, which didn't endear me to the Ab Ex crowd."

"But how could you have said no to a presidential portrait?" Mare asked.

"Not to mention the substantial check." Felix winked at Mare. "Or the prestige."

"Right, right." Elaine looked around for the waiter and exchanged her empty champagne glass for a full one. "Have you seen Felix's Marine Corps Memorial Sculpture, Mare?"

"You're *that* guy?" Mare asked. "The one in Savannah—'The Waving Girl'—right?"

"Yours truly."

"I saw it the first day I walked down to the end of River Street, to the bluff. Really good."

"Why, thank you. So, what else will you girls do while you're in town?"

"Tomorrow I'm taking Mare to see the icons at the Coptic church," Elaine said. "She's working in egg tempera. The Copts use it in their abstract religious paintings."

"Hmm. That's new for you, isn't it?"

"It's not about the religion, Felix. It's about the art."

"No need to apologize, Elaine. You know I'm a huge fan of Michelangelo."

"Yes, and your 'Pietá' is wonderful."

"Pietá?" Mare asked.

"It's a statue of Mary holding the crucified Christ in her lap," Elaine explained. "It hangs in St. Matthew's Cathedral in Washington, D.C."

Mare was again embarrassed at her ignorance, but it felt good to have her professor—with her high standing in the art world— act supportive and use the opportunity to teach in front of this man (Felix Weldon was a *big* deal). Elaine was treating her with respect, so she clearly hadn't brought Mare here to belittle her.

"Say, I have a new religious piece. This way." Felix led them to another room in the gallery, a small alcove with fewer pieces of art. Now it was just the three of them, and Felix stopped in front of a flat, bronze sculpture of the face of Christ which was framed by scenes from his life. A crown of thorns circled his head.

"I call it 'Humanity.'"

"Was this commissioned?" Elaine asked.

"No. But most of my sculptures immortalize people who left an indelible mark on humanity. I thought Jesus should be included."

"It looks kind of like an icon. In bronze," Mare offered.

"Exactly. You've got an observant student here, Elaine." Felix gave them a slight bow. "Well, you girls have a great time. Stay out of trouble here in the big city."

He moved on to mingle with other guests. Elaine and Mare continued to study the exhibit together.

"Felix was one of the first artists to synthesize abstraction and expressionism."

"Is that how the whole Ab Ex thing started?"

"Yes. He believes art should be an outward reflection of the inner self," Elaine said. "But enough lessons for one night. Ready to head back to the hotel?"

"Sure. But give me a minute. I need to use the restroom."

"I'll wait for you outside. I'm dying for a smoke."

As Mare joined Elaine in the parking lot, a couple of kids in dark hoodies hurried around a corner. Mare smelled the aerosol before she saw the graf on the wall of a rundown building near their car. She stared at the words BROKEN PROMISES in large, stenciled letters.

"Does that mean something to you?" Elaine was standing beside Mare now.

"Yeah. That's one of Fekner's mottos."

"Fekner?"

"He's a graf writer up in New York City. First name's John. I'm surprised you didn't hear about him when you lived there."

"I wasn't exactly working on the streets, Mare."

"I know, but Fekner did a lot of protest graf—speaking out against slumlords and city officials who weren't taking care of poor people."

"You know, his name does sound familiar. Seems like he was starting to get attention in respectable art circles. Doing projects about environmental issues?"

"That's him. I guess he's got some followers here in Atlanta." Mare looked wistfully at the wall and the discarded aerosol cans on the ground. When she heard Elaine start the engine, she finally turned away and got into the car.

• • •

The hotel was less than ten minutes away and looked from the outside like a place where the wealthy stayed. Mare followed through the glass front doors behind Elaine and waited while her professor checked in and paid the male desk clerk with a credit card. She avoided his eyes and glanced around the vast lobby, which was almost empty—there were potted plants that looked artificial and prints of wildlife scenes on the walls and a couple of mounted TV sets. Elaine thanked the clerk, and Mare followed her to an elevator, which they took to the eighth floor. They walked down a carpeted hall to their room, which had two double beds with gelatin-silver, print-quilted spreads. A single night table was between them. Elaine tossed her bag onto the luggage rack and headed to the bathroom. "Make yourself comfortable."

Mare was anything but comfortable. She wasn't sure what the rules were. Elaine was paying, so it was like being in her private apartment. Mare sat on the edge of the nearest bed, opened the night table drawer, and pulled out a book. It was the Holy Bible, placed by the Gideons. She opened the cover as Elaine emerged from the bathroom.

"You reading the Bible?"

"I just found it in the drawer. Who are the Gideons?"

"An evangelical group. They've been putting Bibles in hotel rooms for decades."

Mare thumbed through a few pages and stopped at Ephesians 6:1, where a familiar scripture caught her attention: *Children, obey your parents.* Her father's voice crashed into her thoughts. She closed the Bible and placed it back in the drawer.

"Hungry?" Elaine opened her suitcase. "We could order room service. There's the menu next to the phone. Choose something while I change." She stepped back into the bathroom and returned in a robe a minute later. She sat on the bed across from Mare.

"You pick." Mare hated to admit she'd never even stayed in a hotel. "Anything's fine."

They ordered sandwiches, a bottle of wine, and a Coke for Mare. Mare watched Elaine drink a glass of wine and then a second one—on top of the champagne she had at the art gallery. Elaine ate half her sandwich, put the rest on the room service tray, and scooted back against the headboard. She lit a cigarette and coughed several times.

"You okay?" Mare asked.

"I'm fine. Damn smoker's cough. You're awfully quiet tonight. Everything alright?"

"Yeah, sure. This is real nice. I'm just tired."

Elaine smiled. "Got a big day ahead of us tomorrow. Want to get some sleep?"

"Yes." Mare crawled under the covers with her clothes on.

EIGHT

ONCE SHE WAS sure Elaine was in a sound sleep, Mare swung out of bed and reached for her backpack. Being as quiet as she could, she tiptoed to the desk across the room, grabbed one of the two room keys, and held her breath while walking back past Elaine. She eased open the door, looked both ways down the hall and found it clear, then eased the door closed. It clicked into place a lot more loudly than Mare would have preferred, and she cursed silently while imagining Elaine waking up from her stupor inside the room. But maybe the wine right before bed had really knocked her out—Mare didn't hear a sound. She confirmed that the door was locked and started for the bank of elevators.

She reached the ground floor and tried to leave through a back door of the hotel, but it was locked. She went through the lobby and noticed the same desk clerk watching her. He called out as she approached the front door.

"Can I help you?"

Startled, she stopped but didn't turn to face the young man. "No. Thanks."

"It's really not safe to walk in this neighborhood late at night, miss. Are you sure I can't call you a cab?"

"I'll be fine."

"Okay. By the way, the side and back doors of the hotel are closed after ten, so you'll have to enter through the front when you return."

Mare was already out the door before he finished. Based on what he'd just said, hopefully the front doors would be unlocked—she had no clue—but she would worry about that when she returned. The night air (or maybe what was on her mind and had her adrenaline already flowing) led her to pull her hoodie from her backpack and slip her arms into the sleeves. As she strode quickly and put several city blocks between herself and the hotel, she noticed the streets were more and more abandoned and pulled the hood up over her head. She didn't think she'd been gone half an hour when the art gallery parking lot came into view. She flexed her fingers and felt them tingle.

And saw two kids before they saw her.

One was holding up a cardboard stencil while the other filled in the letters with his spray can. Then they backed away and revealed their work: DECAY. Then one of them spotted Mare. Something was said, and they both started to run.

"Wait!" Mare called out. "I'm a writer, too!"

They stopped and turned around. Mare approached slowly, holding her hands at shoulder height, palms toward them.

"What's your name, girl?" the taller one asked.

"Mare. You?"

The first kid looked her over. Then: "I'm Crush. That's LadyP."

Damn! A girl's with him?

"You throwing up work in Atlanta?" Crush asked.

"Not yet ... but I have in—"

"We're about to hit up a boarding house a few blocks away. Wanna help?"

"Uh, I don't have any paint with me ..."

"You can use ours."

"Okay. Sure."

They packed up their supplies, and Mare followed them around a corner and down a few blocks. Each street had buildings more dilapidated than the last, from what Mare could see in the streetlights, and many of those were burned out (or probably shot out). When they arrived at their destination, Mare asked, "What's the deal with this place?"

"We had friends who lived here before they shut it down. Damn landlord wouldn't do shit to keep it open." Crush already had the stencil out and LadyP was shaking a can and handing another one to Mare. "No. Let her help me hold this stencil up."

"We gonna use the big one this time?" LadyP murmured.

"Yeah. This wall can be seen by some of the suits in those offices up there," Crush said, nodding at a skyscraper with a clear view of the building. Mare helped him unfold a large stencil that said THIS WAS SOMEONE'S HOME. LadyP started filling in the letters. The smell of the paint sent a familiar anger surging through Mare's body, as she'd known it would.

• • •

When they were done, Crush asked Mare if she wanted coffee. She followed them to another abandoned building and through a large steel door that slid open. A rat ran across her shoe and she jumped, trying not to scream. Crush laughed and led them into a room with a couple of low-wattage lights.

"Hey, LadyP, take care of her." He started off down a hallway. "I gotta take a leak."

As Mare's eyes adjusted to the semi-darkness, she noticed another kid asleep on the floor. Sleeping bags lined the walls, except for one which had a table stacked high with aerosol cans. There was no kitchen, no coffee pot. Mare was thinking about her safety when LadyP pulled a thermos from her backpack and poured cups for herself and Mare. The caffeine would do her some good, now that the adrenaline rush of the hit was starting to wear off.

"Thanks. You sure you've got enough?"

"Yeah." She sat on the floor near the sleeping kid.

"Never met another female graf writer. How'd you get into this?"

"I was already on the streets when I met Crush and joined his crew."

LadyP couldn't have been more than five feet tall and a hundred pounds dripping wet, but she had a rich, deep voice. She looked up from her coffee and straight into Mare's eyes.

"Had to get away from home. My dad beat the crap out of me when he wasn't doing me or my sister."

"Where was your mother?"

"Now you sound like the welfare people. Too many questions." LadyP got up and pulled something from her backpack. She lit up, took a drag, and offered what was clearly a joint. Mare didn't want this girl to know she hadn't smoked before, so she took a shallow puff without inhaling and handed it back to LadyP.

"Look, I didn't mean—I was homeless, so I wondered what happened to you," Mare said. "You live here? In this building?"

"Sometimes."

"Isn't there a shelter or some place better you can stay?"

"You kidding? Nobody around here cares. So what's your story—*Mare*? That your tag? You a real writer or just a toy?"

This stung. She didn't appreciate this new acquaintance accusing her of being a fake, and she damn sure didn't copy anyone's work. "Shit no! And yes, that's my real name. My tag's Cherry Bomb. I've thrown up a lot of graf."

"Where? I don't remember seeing your work," Crush called out, joining the conversation as he returned.

"You wouldn't have seen my stuff. It was in Macon."

"*Macon*? What's there to hit up in a town like that?"

"It's where I was. I hit up a liquor store and the welfare office. And a church."

"A church? No shit? What was your message, dude?"

Mare regretted having said so much already—she'd just met these two—but she was into the story then and told them about her graf and Lou and *Rolling Stone* and SCAD.

"Yeah ... I remember seeing that piece in *Stone*."

"Sure you did." LadyP laughed a little, checking him now. Mare kept her smile to herself. "During reading hour at the library, right?"

"No, man, some dude had that rag over at a head shop in midtown." Crush cut his eyes at LadyP, then looked back at Mare. "Okay, you did some good work. But now what, you working for the man? I mean, if you ain't protesting, you must've given in."

Mare felt hot blood rush to her face. "Hell no! I just got a chance to study art and get my shit together and have a life. But I miss the streets, man. Not living out here—God, no. But I miss doing graf like crazy."

Crush didn't look like he believed her. But what Mare felt even more was the silence from LadyP this time—it said plenty.

"Looks to me like you've got a nice life now and can't be bothered with changing the world anymore," Crush continued. "What're you doing in Atlanta anyway?"

"One of my professors brought me here for an art show, okay? Earlier tonight."

"Then why you out here with us, Miss Art Student?"

Now Mare felt humiliated. She clenched her fists and tried to blink back tears of anger that had formed—these kids would really howl if she broke down. Telling Crush off wouldn't be smart; they were in an abandoned building the police probably didn't visit unless they had to, and both these kids might have weapons on them or nearby.

Crush didn't wait for a response, however. He told Mare to have a nice life and walked off, laughing to himself. That left Mare with LadyP, who took a deep drag from the joint and looked off into space.

Mare started to speak, but trying to save face at this point just wasn't worth it. She spun on her heels and started back through the building.

NINE

ELAINE WAS JOLTED awake by the door key in the lock. She reached over and flicked on the lamp just as Mare entered the room.

"Mare? My God, I thought someone with the *hotel* was coming in here. Where the hell have you been?" Her voice was gravelly and she started to cough, reaching for the glass of water by her bed. She looked at the alarm clock—just after midnight.

"Oh, sorry to wake you. I was, um, just down the hall looking for a vending machine."

Elaine blinked her eyes and saw what looked like paint in Mare's hair.

"I see. And had the *vending* machine just been painted?"

Elaine's sarcasm scarcely hid her anger. She watched Mare's face but saw no emotion at all. Was she really nonchalant at a time like this or just being a defiant teenager? Mare sighed and sat down on her bed. Elaine could see the paint on her hands as she rubbed them nervously up and down the tops of her thighs, staring at the floor.

"I just ... I just saw those kids with their paint when we were leaving the gallery and it—it said something to me, okay?"

Elaine threw back the covers, stood, lit a cigarette, and took a deep drag. She coughed a bit more before catching her breath. Then, beginning to pace slowly, she turned to look at Mare again. "So, what did you do?"

Mare explained about meeting Crush and LadyP and helping them with their throwup.

"I don't know ... it just brought everything back I've been through," Mare said. "It felt good, being out there. And it was for a good cause! Crush and LadyP were—"

"What were you thinking? Wait—don't answer that. You obviously were not thinking. You were not thinking about your scholarship at SCAD or your future as a real artist—"

"Hey, you have no idea how it feels like to—"

"*Excuse* me, young lady. You were not thinking about the people who have reached out to you and given you the opportunities most kids your age would die for. You could have gotten killed out there tonight! Or badly hurt. Or ended up in jail. Can you at least look at me?"

Mare moved her stare from the floor to Elaine's face, but couldn't hold eye contact for more than a second. When she found her voice again, her words were softer, almost a whisper.

"I'm so sorry. When I saw the graf it was like some sort of drug—I had to get out there."

Elaine put out her cigarette and sat back down on her bed, facing Mare. After pausing to take a deep breath, she spoke in a calmer voice. "I get that Mare, I really do. My husband is an alcoholic, for Pete's sake. And I can't quit these damn smokes. But hanging with these kids who don't have a plan for their lives isn't going to feed that craving you've got."

Elaine paused. Mare didn't say anything, but at least she nodded.

"You can only satisfy that by filling your life with something more meaningful. I was hoping you'd already made that choice when you arrived at SCAD. But if you'd rather run around with your new pal Crush or whoever, I can certainly leave you here ..."

"No!" Now tears were in Mare's eyes, and Elaine felt herself soften. "I told them about SCAD, about you—Crush and LadyP thought I was a fake. Look, I don't want to live on the street. They were passing around a joint ..."

"Do you still want to go to the church to see those icons tomorrow?" Elaine looked into Mare's eyes.

"Yes, if you'll still take me."

"Of course I will. And I really want you to succeed, Mare. But you can't be the SCAD student by day and the street kid—the dope-smoking, hiding-from-the-police-thug—by night. You just can't. Do you understand me?"

"Yes ma'am."

Elaine stubbed her cigarette in the ashtray. She would explore this further with Mare later, but the crisis seemed to be averted for now. "Good. Now go get a shower, then please get back in bed and go to sleep. We have a big day tomorrow."

• • •

Mare headed to the dining room for breakfast while Elaine checked them out at the front desk, giving her some time to reflect on what happened last night. As she sipped coffee and perused the menu, she kept hearing her professor's words in her head. She knew Elaine was right—this was a turning point in her life. She deserved Elaine's anger, considering how nice the woman had been to her. *I can't blow this*, she thought, as Elaine stepped into view and walked to the table.

"Have you ordered yet?" she asked, picking up a menu.

"Just coffee. Waiting for you."

"Hmm ... I'm thinking I'll just have some toast and maybe a little fruit." Elaine closed the menu and looked across at Mare. She didn't look mad, but Mare couldn't quite read what she was seeing.

"Cool. How soon do we need to get on the road?"

"Well, the church is only about fifteen minutes from here, and the woman who answered the phone said it would be open by nine for some sort of prayer service." Elaine looked at her watch. "I thought it would be good to arrive by ten, so we've got twenty minutes or so."

They ate in relative silence, Mare wondering if Elaine was gearing up to start in on her again. She decided to make the first move.

"So, about last night, I want to apologize again." She peered up at Elaine. "And to let you know I'm serious about getting an education and making a better life for myself."

Elaine smiled as she finished chewing a bite of toast. She reached over and touched Mare's arm. "You were lucky last night, and I believe you learned a lesson."

Relief spread through Mare as she took a bite of cantaloupe.

"And please come talk to me any time you're struggling with this, okay?"

Mare returned the smile. "Okay."

• • •

When she and Elaine entered the front doors of Saint Mary of Egypt Coptic Orthodox Church, she smelled incense and heard music—something haunting.

For Mare, whose only experience of church was a makeshift chapel in a barn on a farm, the sheer beauty and otherworldliness of Saint Mary's was overwhelming. Maybe it was more than the art. Maybe it was the incense. The Byzantine chanting. The way the afternoon sun lit up the gold leaf on the icons. Mare recognized some of the figures in the icons from the pictures in the books Elaine had shared with her. Figures from the Old Testament—prophets and kings. Angels. And then scenes from the New Testament—Christ and the apostles, the women at the Cross. None of the sentimental realism of Western art was present. No, something else was at work here.

"You know, I've traveled a lot, but finding this amazing Oriental architecture and art in a church in Georgia is surprising," Elaine whispered. "I don't think this church is very typical for this part of the world."

"And we're probably not typical visitors," Mare whispered back.

A man in a long black robe was standing in the front with his back to the nave, chanting. He had a salt-and-pepper beard and long hair pulled back into a low ponytail. Then he turned, swinging a censer, its smoke billowing toward each of the icons painted on the walls as he circled the room. His steps were slow but decisive.

At one point the priest paused in front of an icon stand. The soft light of candles flickered off the gold leaf in the icon as the priest swung his censer again and bowed. Then he returned to the altar.

Elaine and Mare moved toward the icon and found themselves face to face with an image more powerful than anything Mare had seen before. She drew in a loud breath and whispered to Elaine, "That's her. That's the same woman I saw at the church in Macon—the one who looks like—like my mother."

Elaine looked at Mare and then back at the icon. The woman

in the painting was half-naked, partially covered by an old cloak. Her skin was dark, as though parched by the sun. The figure was almost androgynous. Only skin and bones showed where her right breast should have been (her left side was covered by the cloak) and her face was gaunt. Her shoulder-length hair was unkempt; there were hollow places beneath her eyes. Yet she radiated an undeniable beauty.

"Your *mother*? When did you see her last, Mare?"

"When I was twelve. When we escaped the farm and she left me at the welfare place."

"She just left you there?"

"Yeah, she said she'd come back for me when she got clean. Five years ago. I guess she did the best she could. She didn't have it easy on the farm, either."

Their eyes met.

"I'm not a religious person, Mare." Elaine seemed to struggle to find the words. "Lots of bad stuff happened in my childhood, too."

"May I help you?" The priest had finished the service and slipped up behind them. His voice was calm but direct, and Mare had to hide a smile when Elaine—clearly startled—snapped to attention.

"Oh, yes. Uh, thank you, Father—I'm sorry, what is your name?"

The priest laughed and bowed his head. "Father Mark at your service."

"I'm Elaine de Kooning, and this is Mary Katherine Henry. She's a student at Savannah College of Art and Design, and I'm a visiting professor there. We're here to see the icons—to study them. I've been telling Mare that the iconographers used egg tempera in their work. Also about the Coptic iconographers' style."

"It's nice to meet you both. You've come to the right place, ladies. I should point out to you the spiritual aspects of the icon, as well."

Mare frowned and glanced at Elaine, who started to speak. The priest smiled.

"Don't worry, I'm not going to preach a sermon," he said. "But you both seem taken with this particular icon. Would you like to hear the story behind it?"

They both nodded, and Mare turned her attention to the icon as Father Mark related the story of Saint Mary of Egypt, a fourth-century prostitute who left Alexandria to seek salvation in the desert.

"Mary was only a young girl—probably around twelve years old—when she ran away from her parents to Alexandria. Remember, this was in the fourth century. Life on the streets was much harder then. Mary survived by spinning flax, begging, and prostitution."

"Why did she run away from home?" Mare asked. "Were her parents mean to her?"

"No one knows, although I have often suspected that she was abused as a child. We only know what happened to her in Alexandria, and later in Jerusalem and in the desert. After seventeen years as a harlot, she met some young men who were heading to Jerusalem for a church festival. Mary rode with them on the boat, seducing many of the young men on the voyage."

Mare had been staring at the icon. She turned to the priest. "How do you know all this?"

"Saint Mary told the story herself to a priest she met in the desert. A patriarch—Sophronious—wrote it down later, and it's been a part of churchlore for all these centuries. In fact, in monasteries and many Orthodox churches, her life is read during a service of Great Lent every year. But let me continue her story."

Mare nodded and glanced at Elaine, who smiled back at her.

"When the group reached the church in Jerusalem, Mary tried to follow them inside, but some invisible force prevented her entry. Outside, on the patio, she saw an icon of the Mother of God. She prayed, asking the Mother of God to let her inside the church and promising that she would renounce her sinful ways and do whatever she was told. She had heard that there was a piece of the actual cross that Christ was crucified on inside the church, and she wanted to see this for herself."

Father Mark stood still as he told a story that seemed dear to him. At times, Mare noticed, he would place his fingertips together and rock back and forth on his heels as he spoke, his body keeping rhythm with his words.

"She was finally permitted to enter the church, where she venerated the cross and had a conversion experience. Afterward, she went into the desert to live as a hermit for another seventeen years. Finally a priest, Father Zosimas, found her when he was on a private retreat in the desert. He became convinced she was a saint because of several miracles she performed. When he returned to the desert a year later, she was dead. A lion helped him bury her."

"That's kinda hard to believe," Mare murmured. She felt tears in her eyes and tried to blink them back. "I'm just sayin' ..."

Father Mark nodded. "Indeed it is. But church history is full of miracles and stories of people's lives being changed dramatically."

"You okay?" Elaine asked gently.

"What? Sure." Mare wiped her face with the back of her hand. "Just kind of musty in here, or something."

Elaine looked at her watch. "We must go. I need to prepare for a lecture. And you need time in the studio."

"Yeah, I do. Um, you mind if I ask Father Mark something? I'll meet you in the car."

• • •

Mare was surprised at how comfortable she felt being alone with Father Mark. Something in his countenance invited trust. She looked at his kindly face and asked what was in her heart.

"I really want to learn more about icons—how to paint them, if that's possible. Or is that something only religious people do?"

"Sure, if you're serious about this, Mare. There's a nun who teaches icon classes at a monastery in North Carolina. In fact, there's one coming up the week of the Feast Day of Saint Mary of Egypt."

"She has a feast day? What's that?"

"Most saints in the Catholic and the Orthodox church have a day on the calendar each year when the church remembers them. It's usually the date of their death. The nuns at this monastery have a special devotion to Saint Mary. So every year they host an icon workshop just before her feast day."

"Is it just for Orthodox people?" Mare asked.

"No. Anyone can take the class. Are you interested?"

"Yes. I mean, I think so. I probably need to talk to Elaine about it since she's my advisor at school."

• • •

"What was so moving about that icon, Mare?" Elaine asked a few minutes after they'd gotten back on the road for Savannah. Mare had noticed her professor's silence as they left the church—it wasn't like Elaine de Kooning to be quiet for very long.

"Oh, you know—it's like I told you—reminds me of my mother."

"Physically? I mean, is that what your mother looked like?"

"Not exactly. Something in the eyes—can't explain it."

Mare watched the landscape fly past. Wildflowers hemmed the edge of the road. Empty fields stretched for miles. Weathered fences defined the scattered farms. As they approached Macon, the occasional train track took Mare back to her childhood, to those freight cars she saw in Forsyth—the ones with graffiti on them. And the scratchy sounds of Uncle Miles' radio, playing Randy Newman's "Kingfish" and Billy Joe Shaver's "I Been to Georgia on a Fast Train." She remembered wondering if the train that passed near their house could take her away from the nightmare. Elaine's voice brought her back to the present.

"So, what did you and Father Mark discuss?"

"If he knew of someone around here who gives lessons in painting icons."

"And what did he say?"

"He knows about a workshop," Mare said.

The empty fields gave way to dense woods. Dirt roads zigzagged through the trees, like the road that led to Uncle Miles and Aunt Sue's house. A truck left a cloud of dust as it disappeared into the trees. Mare followed its path with her eyes.

"Where?"

"In North Carolina—at a monastery. A nun there teaches iconography."

Elaine took so long to respond that Mare looked over at her. "You wouldn't seriously consider going there, would you?"

"Not to be a nun, Elaine. I might like to paint icons. I was just thinking about it ..."

"It seems kind of extreme, Mare."

Mare hesitated. "He said there's a weeping icon there."

"Weeping?"

"Yeah, like tears coming out of its eyes. A sweet-smelling oil. I know—it sounds weird. He called it 'myrrh-streaming.' He said a nun at the monastery painted it. She had been abandoned as a child, abused for most of her life. So she came to the monastery for shelter."

"How do they know it's not some kind of hoax?"

"Some bishops validated it. Said the tears were real. It was all over the newspapers and everything. People came from miles around to see it. And to pray for healing."

"So now you've got your hopes up for some out-of-this-world religious experience. To take away your pain, right?"

Mare looked out the window. *First you yell at me for hanging out with street kids, and now you're unhappy about me wanting to visit a monastery. What do you want from me?* But she was too exhausted for another confrontation and let it drop, hoping Elaine would, too. They breezed past a road sign that said MACON THREE MILES.

"Hey, Elaine, do we have time to stop in Macon? Someone there I'd like to see."

"Macon? Who do you know there? Lou Lieberman went back to New York, remember?"

"You might not understand—"

"Fine. What do you want to see?"

"Well, that icon in the church where I threw up that last graf piece—I saw a painting of Mary, that Egyptian. I just want to look at it again, that's all."

Elaine didn't answer, but she took the exit for Macon. Mare directed her to the church. They passed the coffee shop where Mare first met Lou, where her emancipation began. A lump formed in her throat remembering those days—and strengthened her resolve to move forward in a positive way.

• • •

Elaine pulled into the parking lot at St. Joseph Catholic Church and killed the engine. She studied the mural. "I guess that's the mural you helped paint, right?"

"Yeah. It's kind of embarrassing," Mare admitted. "You don't have to come in, unless you want to meet Father Joseph."

"It's alright. I'd like to come in."

As they entered the church, Mare remembered her fear in meeting Father Joseph after her graffiti hit. But she remembered something more—her attraction to the icon of Mary of Egypt. She wanted to see it again and talk with Father Joseph about it.

"Mare! Come in!" Father Joseph welcomed them as they entered his office. "I'm so pleased to see you."

"I hope I'm not interrupting you."

"And who is this?"

"Oh, sorry. This is Elaine de Kooning. She's my teacher—my professor at SCAD."

"Ms. de Kooning. It's an honor. You and your husband are legends in the Ab Ex world. I'm sure the college over at Savannah must be proud to have you on faculty."

Elaine looked stunned. "You know my work?"

"Of course. I went to seminary just outside Manhattan in the late '50s. Whenever I could, I would sneak to the city to take in the art scene. A nice balance for my theological studies. So, what brings you ladies here today?"

"We—well, *I* really came to see the icon again," Mare said. "Is it okay to go into the church?"

"Certainly. I'll go with you. It's almost time to pray the None."

"The *None*?"

"The prayers we say at the ninth hour, usually around three p.m. It doesn't last long—a few Psalms and a few short prayers."

Mare and Elaine followed Father Joseph into the church, where he showed them the candles that parishioners often lit when entering.

"Would you like to light one?" He offered a long beeswax taper to Mare, and another one to Elaine.

Mare looked at Father Joseph. "I'm not Catholic, remember."

Father Joseph laughed lightly. "You don't have to be Catholic to pray, Mare. God hears everyone. The candles help us remember we are in His presence. Like the incense and the icons. All these things appeal to our physical senses."

Mare fingered her taper. Something about the way the beeswax gave to her slightest touch softened her heart, so she lit the taper and placed it in the sand near the icon of Saint Mary of Egypt. "Is it okay if I just stand here while you do the prayers?"

"Sure."

Elaine lit her taper and placed it beside Mare's. Then Father Joseph walked to the front of the church and raised his hands in prayer. At one point he opened a prayer book and read from several Psalms, including Psalm 126. Elaine and Mare heard his words from the back of the nave:

When the Lord brought back the captives to Zion,

We were like those who dream.

Mare found herself wondering who the captives were, and what Zion was. The words were vaguely familiar. Maybe she remembered her father talking about Zion, back on the farm. Wasn't that where he told everyone they would go during the final ceremony—the one that she and her mother escaped? This brought back bad memories, and she started to turn and leave just as Father Joseph read more of the Psalm:

Restore our fortunes, O Lord ...

Those who sow in tears will weep with songs of joy.

Mare stopped and looked at the face of Mary of Egypt. She could see where the iconographer had indicated the tracks of her tears. Why was Mary weeping? Was the icon at the monastery actually weeping real tears? Or oil, as Father Mark had said? She was so enrapt with the icon that she didn't notice Elaine standing beside her—Elaine's eyes had tears in them. Father Joseph finished the prayers and joined them.

"She wept for her sins."

"Really?" Mare felt anger ripple through her. She whirled to face the priest. "Is that all?"

"I'm not sure what you mean."

"Well, I know she was a prostitute and all that, but what about what happened to her when she was a kid? Who pays for those sins? It doesn't seem fair."

"No, it's not fair," Father Joseph said quietly. "But is childhood abuse an excuse for sin? And no one knows for sure what happened to her as a child."

"How about abandonment? Does that count?"

"Your parents will answer to God one day for what they did to you, Mare. But until then, you need to find a way to forgive them, to be an adult. Or the anger will destroy you."

Mare was trying to take this in while reminding herself that Father Joseph clearly cared about her—he'd been every bit as supportive as Lou and Margaret—when Elaine turned and strode off without a word.

"Is she all right?" Father Joseph asked Mare.

"I guess so. She's not really into religion. She probably just went to wait for me in the car." Mare faced the priest. "Can I ask you something?"

"Sure. What is it?"

"Do you know Father Mark, in the Coptic Church in Atlanta?"

"Yes, we've met."

"Well, Elaine took me to his church to see the icons today, and he told me there's an icon of Mary of Egypt at a monastery in North Carolina that weeps. I want to see it."

"Hmm. That could be quite an eventful experience, Mare. Can you take time off from school to make the pilgrimage?"

"Well, he said they offer iconography workshops there. I want to apply for a scholarship from SCAD to take one. It's only for a week."

"I've never seen a weeping icon—it would be worth the trip. To study iconography while you're there would be purposeful." Father Joseph smiled one of his signature smiles, and Mare imagined a kindly father or grandfather. She sure didn't have one of her own.

"Thank you, Father. And I'm sorry about getting worked up. Just hits close to home."

"You ask good questions, Mare. I'm always here if you want to talk, or ask anything."

Elaine was pacing in the parking lot when Mare came out of the church a minute later. She saw Mare, dropped her cigarette and crushed it with her shoe, and climbed into her car. Mare got into the passenger seat.

"I'm sorry I took so long, Elaine. Are you okay?"

"Of course I'm okay. I just need to get back to the school. I have work to do."

Mare took a long look at her professor, who stared straight ahead.

TEN

ELAINE RETURNED TO her carriage house in Savannah to prepare for another week of lectures and studio classes at SCAD. Her hopes of mentoring a promising student were now complicated by Mare's new religious bent and her own stirrings—she almost regretted taking her to Atlanta. All this talk about monasteries ... and North Carolina. Elaine found herself spending more time reflecting on some of the dark secrets of her past.

Trying to drown those secrets with booze didn't work, and she found herself too depressed to face her students one day that week, so she canceled studio. Somehow it didn't occur to her that Mare would drop by her office to check on her, and she walked in right in the middle of Elaine spending what she'd thought was a private moment looking over several paintings she'd spread out on the floor. She never bothered to frame them or even stretch them on canvas frames. The raw edges were frayed, just like the edges of her life.

Elaine scowled, quickly rolled up the paintings, and placed them in a cabinet behind her desk. She stood with her back to Mare and cleared her throat.

"Do you ever knock?"

"I was just checking on you. You weren't there today, and—what were those paintings?"

Elaine turned around to reach for a tissue. Her eyes were red and swollen.

"Are you all right? What's wrong?"

"Close the door, Mare, and sit down, please. There's something I need to tell you. And I'm pretty sure you're going to be angry with me."

"Why?" Mare quietly eased the door shut, then pulled a chair close to Elaine's desk. She sat and leaned on the desk with her elbows, her hands clasped under her chin. Her eyes were full of curiosity.

"I did those paintings about thirty-five years ago. During a summer I spent near Black Mountain, North Carolina."

"Hey, that's—that's close to the monastery where the icon classes are taught, isn't it?"

"Yes. Your plans got me started thinking about that summer again. I went there to an artist colony, to paint."

"Cool! But … why would that make you so sad—and me angry?"

Elaine looked down at her desk, unable to face Mare as she continued. "I also went there to have a baby."

"I didn't know you had children. You've never mentioned them."

"No, I haven't. That's because I only had the one child. A girl.

I left her in an orphanage in North Carolina and went back to New York alone."

Elaine watched Mare's face for the judgment she feared she would see. Why did it matter so damn much to her what this student thought? She could no longer deny that she was drawn to something in Mare's person—something that made her care about her more than her other students. And to care what Mare thought about *her*.

"Okay ... what did your husband think?"

"He didn't know, Mare. It wasn't his child. Willem and I had been separated on and off. Both of us had had numerous affairs. It was just part of who we were back then."

"So was she adopted or what?"

"No. I couldn't bear to lose her forever—I wouldn't sign the release papers. I told the social worker I would come back for her, you know, when things in New York were different."

"What do you mean, 'when things were different'?"

"The art scene in New York. It was a difficult place for a woman in those days, Mare. I was struggling in my husband's shadow. I couldn't be saddled with the cares of motherhood. Not then. Not yet."

"So when *did* you go back for her?"

The question hung in the air. Finally Elaine looked at Mare. "I didn't."

"So she grew up in an orphanage. And you had a great time pursuing your career. How could you do that?"

Mare got up to leave. Elaine reached across the desk and grabbed her arm. Their eyes met. Elaine was afraid she would lose Mare with this revelation—she could take the girl's *pain*, but it was her *anger* that scared her most of all, and what she saw then in Mare's face was anger.

"What was her name?" Mare's voice was barely more than a whisper.

"Lily. Well, that was her nickname. Her real name was Susannah Grace."

"And you never looked for her?"

Shame invaded Elaine's soul with these words. She could barely stand to look at Mare as she tried to explain. "No. I've thought about it. Many times over the years. But it's been so long now. It seems too difficult."

"Well. So what happened to her? Was she ever adopted?"

"No. She lived in the orphanage until ..."

"Until what, Elaine?"

"She ran away, Mare. There were rumors of abuse at the orphanage. From the priests there. Even the sisters—the nuns."

"No wonder you haven't wanted to visit those churches with me, or talk with Father Mark or Father Joseph."

"I can only imagine what her life was like. I cannot forgive myself for not going back for her. Then when I heard about you and what you had been through, well—at first I wanted to keep you at arm's length."

"And now?" Mare's eyes asked the question as much as her words.

"Now I can only try to be your friend. I don't deserve your forgiveness, Mare, but I keep hoping."

"So, where has she been all these years, your daughter?"

"I don't know. The authorities never found her. There's a good chance she died somewhere on the streets. It was the seventies—lots of hippies and drugs."

"How old would she be?"

"Now? Thirty-four."

Again the silence found them. Elaine couldn't bear it for more than a few seconds. She moved closer and tried to touch Mare on the arm, but Mare pulled away.

"Please. I knew you would be angry. But I had to tell you."

"Why *me*? Why didn't you tell Father Joseph or Father

Mark? They hear confessions all the time. Maybe they can forgive you. Maybe they can even convince you that God forgives you. But not me. I can't stand to be anywhere near you. I'm leaving SCAD."

"No. You don't need to do that, Mare. I've already given notice. I'm leaving when the fall semester is over. My husband is sick and needs me back in New York. You won't have to be around me much longer—just one more semester. And I can arrange for you to be in someone else's studio class if you'd rather."

This seemed to cool Mare's anger for the moment. "Sick? What's wrong with him?"

"He's a drug addict. An alcoholic. He's also losing his memory. The doctors think it's Alzheimer's," Elaine said. "I need to be with him. In fact, I'm planning on visiting him soon. During Christmas holidays." She paused. "What are you doing during winter break?"

Mare shrugged and backed away from the desk. Suddenly Elaine realized that Mare didn't have anywhere to go for the holidays. *This can't get any worse.*

"I'll probably go home with a friend who lives in Atlanta."

"Really? Who?"

"Oh, you don't know her. She's not in your class."

Elaine could tell that Mare was lying but didn't want to press her. She had thrown enough emotional baggage at her for one day. She didn't say anything when Mare spun and left the room without a word.

ELEVEN

MARE HAD LIED to Elaine about going home with a friend for the Christmas holidays. She hadn't made any real friends at SCAD. But she did catch a ride with Kimberly Pittman—the rich girl from Buckhead.

"I guess so," Kimberly had said when Mare asked about it. "I mean, my dad is sending a car for me, but we can probably make room for you. If you only bring one bag."

Her snobbery put Mare off, and the 250-mile drive was awkward, but she was desperate and played the part of the humble homeless kid—she didn't even have to pretend when she saw the brand-new, shiny black 1983 Chrysler Executive. Kimberly's driver, a man named Thomas, was older and didn't speak unless spoken to. He wore a navy blue uniform that included a cap.

"What are you going to do while you're in Atlanta?" Kimberly said after introducing them. She was burying herself in a fashion magazine even as she asked the question.

"Oh, I don't know. Visit some friends. Maybe work on some art stuff." Mare looked out the window, away from Kimberly. Leaving SCAD reminded her of the trip with Elaine a few weeks earlier. "What about you?"

"The usual. Mom and Dad will have their huge Christmas Eve party. My brother and sister and all our old friends will be there." She looked across the seat at Mare. "Oh, that was inconsiderate of me. I'm sure you're missing your family at this time of the year."

Like you give a rip, honey.

Mare didn't bother with a response. She reached into the pocket of her hoodie for her earplugs and put them in her ears, then turned on her Walkman. Leaning her head against the window, she hoped Kimberly would get the message that there was no further need for conversation. A few lines into Culture Club's "Do You Really Want to Hurt Me" and she was in her own world. Then she was asleep.

• • •

"Mare. Wake up. We're coming into Atlanta. Where should Thomas drop you off?" Kimberly was brushing her hair and putting on lipstick, leaning over the back of the front passenger seat to check herself in the mirror.

"What ... oh, yeah. I don't know the address. I mean—my friend is going to meet me at a hotel downtown. It's the Regency Hyatt House. On Peachtree."

Thomas caught Mare's eyes in his rearview mirror and nodded.

"The Regency?" Kimberly looked shocked.

"I know. What's an orphan like me doing in a swanky place like that?"

Kimberly blushed. Mare kept her smile to herself. "I'm sorry. I didn't mean ..."

Yes you did. "I'm not staying there. We're going to look at some art galleries nearby. It was just an easy place to meet."

As they approached the hotel, Mare rolled down her window and looked up at the iconic blue saucer—the Polaris Restaurant—which sat atop the hotel's twenty-two floors. She could appreciate the genius of Atlanta's homeboy, the architect John Portman, who designed the Polaris and many other buildings in the business district.

"There it is." Mare signaled for Thomas to pull to the curb. Thanks for the ride." She turned to Kimberly, who was still touching up her hair. "See you in a couple of weeks."

"You've got my parents' phone number?"

"Yeah. Thanks."

Mare hopped out, turned to grab her backpack from the seat, and returned Thomas' smile to be polite. The traffic light was red, though, leaving Mare standing there feeling awkward—now she had to go into the hotel to save face. The lobby took her breath away. She had seen pictures of it in a magazine, but they didn't really capture its glamour—wallpaper with raised velvet ribbons adorned the walls; a huge crystal chandelier hung from a vaulted ceiling. A doorman in a dark blue suit eyed her hoodie, black jeans, and boots. Then he approached with an official-looking stance.

"May I help you, miss?"

"Uh, no. I'm good." She started to walk deeper into the lobby, but the doorman stepped in front of her.

"Are you staying here?"

"What do you care?"

"The hotel lobby is only for the use of our guests and patrons of the restaurant."

"I just need to pee and I'll be out of here."

"I'm sorry, miss. The restrooms are also reserved for our customers."

Mare could feel the heat rising as her face turned red. "Jesus, man. I've been on the road for hours and I'm meeting a friend. Can I just take a leak? Please?"

The doorman ushered Mare to the back of the lobby and pointed down a hallway. "The ladies room is just past the elevator on the right."

Once she was safely inside the restroom she stopped to look at herself in the mirror. She hadn't brushed her hair after napping with her hoodie on during the trip from Savannah—she hadn't bothered with makeup or even a clean shirt. After using the toilet she freshened up at the sink. A couple of ladies in fancy clothes came out of two of the stalls and stared and whispered as they left the restroom. Mare hadn't even felt this out of place at the art gallery with Elaine and Felix Weldon.

She hurried through the lobby, dodging the doorman and keeping her head down. Once outside she took a deep breath and looked up and down the street to get her bearings. She thought she could find her way back to the neighborhood where LadyP and Crush hung out. A few blocks in one direction, and then another, and finally she was looking at one of the buildings with the stencil graf on it. Their hangout was nearby, wasn't it? Yes ... just down that alley. She started that way, then stopped.

Suddenly her stomach was doing flips.

Why had she lied to Elaine about coming to Atlanta? *Why am I even here?* She'd told Elaine she was done with graf, but was it a sense of unfinished business with LadyP? Mare didn't care if she ever saw Crush again, but she braced herself for that possibility as she knocked on the large metal door. She looked up and down the alley. No one was around ... and there was no answer to her knock.

"Crush! LadyP! It's Mare!"

Once it was clear no one was inside (or was going to answer), she turned and leaned her back against the door. She crossed her arms and looked warily up and down the alley. *What a stupid-as-shit thing to do. Like they'd even speak to me anyway.* Her stomach growled, and she tried to remember the cheap café she'd seen the last time she was here. She walked six or seven blocks, not completely sure she was going the right way, and found it nestled between an old thrift store and several places that were boarded up. It was the middle of the afternoon and there were no other customers inside. She slid into a booth by the window. A moment later a tired-looking older woman walked out from behind the counter and handed her a menu.

"We're out of mashed potatoes."

"What?" Mare hadn't even looked at the menu yet.

"Today's lunch. You get a meat and two vegetables. But we're out of potatoes."

"Oh, that's okay." She looked at the menu. Her stomach growled again, audibly. The waitress smiled.

"How 'bout the blue plate special? Chicken fried steak, green beans, and okra."

"That's fine."

"Cornbread?"

"Please."

When her food arrived, Mare devoured it quickly. The waitress brought a refill of sweet tea after a while. Nobody else had set foot in the place. It smelled like fried meat in here, and she figured she could eat another plate before getting full.

"You live around here?"

"I, um, no. I go to school in Savannah. I'm just visiting some friends for the holidays."

"Sure you are, honey. Bet they live in a nice house in Buckhead, too."

"What's it to you, lady?" Mare snapped.

"Sorry. Didn't mean to hit a nerve. You really a student in Savannah?"

"Yeah, an art student."

"Well, that explains it, then."

"Explains *what*?"

"The clothes. And the paint under your fingernails."

This, at least, sounded kind. Mare looked at her empty plate, then up at the waitress. She was probably seventy or more, with gray hairs that mingled with the strings of brown that crept out of the bun on top of her head. A torn hairnet was barely hanging on with two black bobby pins and a pencil stuck through the middle of the bun. But her skin was smooth and her eyes were soft. She smiled, looking in that moment like a beloved grandmother, and suddenly Mare was fighting back tears. The waitress sat down in the booth and reached across the tabletop for Mare's hand. Mare let her hold it for a long moment before pulling it back and wiping her face.

"Do you need a place to stay?"

Mare nodded.

Taking a deep breath and looking out the window, the waitress furrowed her brow. "There's a shelter a couple of miles from here. Not a great neighborhood, but they don't turn anyone away. You can catch a bus up at the corner and it will take you within a block or two of the place. I'll write down the address for you." She pulled the pencil from her hair and scribbled on a piece of paper from her order pad. She tore it off and handed it to Mare.

"Thanks," Mare whispered. "How much for the lunch?"

"It's on the house, honey. Be careful out there."

CHERRY BOMB

• • •

The city bus—with MARTA painted broadly on the side—pulled up to the corner just as Mare arrived at the stop. She handed the address to the driver. He looked at Mare with a bored expression and motioned for her to sit down. The bus smelled rank, and Mare took a seat close to the driver and kept her eyes averted from nearby passengers. The last time she had been on a bus, she thought as it pulled into traffic, was when she ran away from Forsyth for Macon last summer. A lot had happened since then, and yet here she was on her own again. Why hadn't she stayed on campus during the holidays? The dorms and the cafeteria were open for international students and others who didn't have family nearby. It would have been safe. Was LadyP worth the risk she was taking? Or was that *really* what this little jaunt to Atlanta was about?

The bus driver interrupted her thoughts. "This is it, miss. Your stop. The place you're looking for is right down there." He pointed down the street to a single-story brick building.

Mare stepped off the bus and threw on her backpack. As the bus drove away she felt a chill in the air so she zipped her jacket and pulled her hoodie over her head. It was a short walk to the shelter but it felt like a long journey. She stood in front of the door staring at the dirt lining the sidewalk on both sides—grass should have been growing there, even in December. The shrubs in front of the building were shaggy and did little to hide the crumbling building behind them. Loose shingles hung from the edges of the roof. Duct tape and cardboard covered over a missing windowpane. What had she gotten herself into?

Inside the shelter the sights weren't much better, although it was warm. There was an old wooden desk in the foyer with a hand printed-sign that read PLEASE RING THE BELL. A small metal bell with a button on top sat next to the sign. Mare could hear noises coming from down a hallway as she rang the bell. After a minute a tall man came through the double doors from the hallway, staring at the floor as he walked.

"We're full, dude."

Mare pulled her hoodie back, revealing her streaked blond hair and a face that couldn't belong to a dude.

"Oh. Sorry. I thought—well, we mostly get men in here."

"Do you take women?"

"Yeah. Lately I've given away some of the rooms on the women's side to men, but there are a couple left. My name's Henry. I'm the resident manager."

"I'm Mare. Any other women staying here right now?"

"Only two. You want a bed?"

"How much?" Mare set her backpack on the desk and unzipped one of the small sections and pulled out her wallet.

"It's paid for by the city."

Mare couldn't believe her ears. "It's free? People live here for free?"

"Well, they don't exactly live here. You can only stay for two weeks at a time unless you can show proof of employment. Then you can stay for six months. We got programs that help you get housing after that."

After Mare showed Henry her driver's license and filled out several minutes' worth of paperwork, he led her down a hall that ran to the left of the front desk—the opposite direction from the double doors through which he had entered earlier.

"This is supposed to be the women's hall, but we got a few dudes living in some of these rooms just 'cause I couldn't turn them away," he said. They stopped in front of a closed wooden door with a small number 5 glued on it. Henry unlocked the door and handed Mare the key. "Let me know if you need anything."

She thanked him and watched him start back for the front. Then she stepped in and flipped on the light. It was daytime, but the only window was near the ceiling and the room was dim. The gray-green concrete block walls were cracked and the old linoleum flooring was torn and peeling. It made her place back in Savannah look like a castle. More regrets set in when she realized all at once how badly she needed to use the bathroom. *Must be down the hall.* She dropped her backpack on the floor and started out her door just in time to catch a young woman entering a room a couple of doors down.

"Hey! Excuse me! Can you tell me where the bathrooms are?"

It took a second, but the woman—barely more than a girl—stepped back into view. Mare froze, wondering if she'd seen a ghost.

"*LadyP?!?*"

"Yeah, it's me," she said crossly. "What the hell are you doing here?"

"Long story. First I need to pee. Where's the john?"

LadyP pointed down the hall. "Last door on the left."

Mare found the grimy bathroom, did her business, and found her way back to LadyP's room. The door was open.

"Don't just stand there, *Mare.* Come on in."

There was an aluminum folding chair next to the bed. LadyP pointed to it, and Mare crossed the room and sat down. LadyP plopped down on the bed, which bounced and made a loud creaking sound. "Yeah, I know. Pretty crappy here."

"No. I wasn't thinking that," Mare lied.

"Sure you weren't. Bet you live in a really nice place over at that highfalutin' school."

"It's all right ... okay, it's really nice."

"How are classes?"

"They're ... good. I mean, I'm learning a lot. And there's this one teacher who's been real nice to me, but ..."

"But *what?*" LadyP sat up on the edge of her bed and leaned forward, elbows on her thighs, cradling her face in her palms.

131

"Well, I miss doing graffiti. The excitement."

"Not all it's cracked up to be."

"Yeah, I get that. And I told Elaine—my professor—that I wasn't going to do it anymore."

"Yet here you are, *Mare*."

"I'm not really sure why I'm here. Guess I wanted to find you."

"*Me*? Why?"

"You reminded me of something I missed, I suppose." Mare found it hard to find the right words. "Your courage, I guess ... trying to fight the slumlords and all that. Seemed like a good thing."

LadyP made a snorting sound. Mare wasn't sure if she picked up sadness or scorn. "I don't know if we've done any good or not."

"Well. So where's Crush?"

"He split. Found some toy who claimed to know a crew in New York looking for new talent, so he took off."

"I'm sorry."

"Screw him. Who needs that asshole, anyway." LadyP stood. Mare couldn't read what was on her face. Then, without warning, LadyP leaned down—suddenly their lips met in a soft, short kiss. Horrified at the ripple of desire she felt, Mare jumped to her feet and backed a step away, then another. Then she turned her back and started for the door.

"Don't leave."

Mare turned and faced her, still feeling the hot blood in her face. "What was that?"

"It was what it was." LadyP took a step closer.

"I don't want you ... not like that."

"You got a guy back at school, huh?"

"No. Nothing like that." Mare tried to think how to say what she was feeling. "It's just ... I don't think I'm into girls, either. I need some time to figure out who I am."

"Come on, sit down." LadyP moved back to the bed and pointed at the chair. She grabbed a pack of Winstons and a cheap lighter from the nightstand, pulled out a cigarette and lit up, sending smoke into the air. "I won't touch you again, promise."

"Give me one of those," Mare said.

"Didn't know you smoked," LadyP replied, but lit a second one and handed it over.

"Haven't for long. How old are you, anyway?"

"Nineteen. You?"

"Sixteen," Mare admitted.

"Jesus. How'd you get into that college so young?"

"They let me take the GED. It was mainly about my art, the scholarship and all that. And I do want to finish school. But, damn, it's hard to get the graf out of my system."

"I hear ya. Hey, I'm going to meet up with a new crew tonight. I've heard they're planning some cool throwups. Want to come?

Mare hesitated. She was still mad at Elaine, but was this a good way to deal with it? Was the excitement of one night on the streets with LadyP worth risking her career—which Elaine seemed to think Mare had ahead of her?

"Yeah. I'm in."

"Cool. They serve supper here at six. We can grab some free grub and then head over to meet the crew."

• • •

It was dark and getting chilly outside when Mare and LadyP left the shelter. Mare hadn't done graffiti in the winter, and she muttered that her hands were already cold before they'd even reached the site.

"Here." LadyP pulled an extra pair of gloves out of her backpack and handed them to Mare. "You can't paint well if your fingers are frozen."

Mare pulled the gloves on as they walked. She noticed the

fingers had been cut off for a better grip on cans or markers. "Thanks."

It took about fifteen minutes to get to the meet-up location. The first thing Mare noticed was that all the other taggers were male. She gave LadyP a wary look. LadyP gave her a chin-up as they approached the group. The tallest guy spoke first.

"Who's the chick?"

"This is Mare. She's got experience. I thought we could use another pair of hands. This is Twist."

Twist looked at Mare but didn't speak to her.

"Just keep her close to you," he said to LadyP. "I don't have time to babysit anybody. Now listen up, everyone: We've got a new target tonight. That crew over in midtown—GMan's guys—they've been biting our work. They've thrown up some new pieces down in Castleberry Hill, that neighborhood where they're converting old warehouses into condos and shit. I've heard it looks way too much like our style. We need to head down there and take it out."

A short guy in a muscle shirt with tat-covered arms spoke up. "That's over a mile away, Twist."

"What are you whining about now, Demon? Hell, it's only a twenty-minute walk."

"Why would they do that?" LadyP asked. "I mean, they trying to make it look like your work, Twist?"

"Maybe. Some of GMan's people got arrested or some shit like that."

"What was their message?" Mare asked.

Twist stared at her as though she were an alien. Then he walked over to Mare and leaned down until they were practically nose to nose. "Did I ask you to talk to me?"

LadyP stepped over next to Mare. "She's got a right to ask, Twist."

"That's just it," Twist snarled, directing his answer to LadyP rather than to Mare. "GMan and his crew don't have a message of their own. That's why they bite ours."

It all sounded very childish to Mare, but she was there now, so she decided to shut up and just go along with the plan. And if Twist—who seemed to have a pretty short fuse—or one of these other boys got physical with her or LadyP, she didn't know how they'd defend themselves.

Twist had apparently said all he was going to say, though, and they walked quietly along the dark city blocks until Twist held up his hand for them to stop. They were in front of one of the warehouses now.

"Shit. This looks like a crappy version of our work."

Mare squinted, trying to make out the design and tags in the glow of the dim streetlights. Twist turned to one of the guys and said, "You got the white paint and rollers?"

The guy nodded and began handing out rollers out to the other men.

"What about us?" LadyP asked.

"Too dangerous. Let us do the cross-outs. You two can help with the new throw-up."

Mare watched as Twist and the others piled up some old crates and climbed up on them to reach the graf with their rollers. The graf that had been there swiftly disappeared in a sea of white paint. Mare, now eager to be involved, was about to step forward when LadyP gasped.

"Twist! Watch out!"

Mare whirled and saw a throng of boys rounding a corner and sprinting into view. Fear coursed through her, but her legs felt glued to the sidewalk. This was obviously the crew who'd done the throwup, and they pushed the boys off their makeshift scaffolding and hit them with their aerosol cans. Twist, momentarily knocked off his feet, jumped up and into the face of the biggest, oldest-looking crew member.

"What the hell, GMan? You want to front us?"

"You're buffing our work, asshole!"

"That's how it's done, man. It's not about violence. You and your guys are a bunch of thugs."

GMan responded with a lightning-quick punch to the jaw that knocked Twist off his feet, and Mare was about to grab LadyP's hand and start running when a shot to her own head nearly brought her to her knees.

"What the *fuck* are you doing?" LadyP said, suddenly in front of Mare and trying to shield her.

"Shit. Didn't know she was a damned *girl*."

Mare blinked her eyes and took in as much air as she could, trying to get her wits about her. She was in serious trouble if the guy who'd conked her with his aerosol can came after her, but he turned to fight someone else. Then she felt movement and saw LadyP back a step away. Suddenly she was running, Mare right behind her. They didn't stop until they were several blocks away and well out of view of the street fight. They collapsed on the sidewalk, Mare's hands just inches from a pile of broken glass, and leaned up against the concrete wall of a warehouse. She heard sirens nearby.

"You okay?" LadyP was on her knees at Mare's side. "How's your head? Can you get back to the shelter?"

"Guess I'll have to," Mare said. It throbbed and was painful to the touch, but she didn't see any blood on her fingers.

• • •

Henry was at the front desk when Mare followed LadyP into the shelter. "Jesus. What happened?"

"Can we just have some ice, please?" LadyP asked.

"Sure. Come on in the kitchen."

Mare sat heavily on a folding chair in front of a scuffed wooden table, faintly aware of the smell of spoiled food—maybe the garbage needed taking out. Henry opened a freezer and grabbed an ice tray. He popped out a bunch of cubes, put them in a kitchen towel, and handed it to LadyP. Mare let LadyP pull her hoodie back and examine her head.

"No blood—"

"Good."

"—just a large ugly bump. Here." She put the towel in Mare's hands and stepped back. Mare pressed it gently to the bump, then more firmly.

"So, y'all gonna tell me what happened?" Henry asked.

Mare wasn't about to explain. It was LadyP's great idea—she could get into it.

"Uh, these two crews got into a fight and we were sort of stuck in the middle."

"Should I call the cops?"

"Hell, no." LadyP looked up at Henry. "Besides, we heard sirens as we left, so I'm sure they're all over it by now. Hey, can we have some water or something?"

"Sure, but this discussion isn't over. We can't have trouble here at the shelter."

Henry stayed with them until he thought Mare had survived without a concussion. Mare was silent the whole time, thinking back over the choices she'd made on this trip and tried to imagine Elaine's reaction ... and those of Margaret, Lou, and Father Joseph. LadyP told Henry she'd come get him if Mare started getting sick, and with that the girls started for their rooms. LadyP followed Mare into her room, and for a second Mare wondered if LadyP was going to put the moves on her again. But she remained on her feet when Mare sat on the bed, and she offered a cigarette after lighting up. Mare didn't hesitate and held her first puff in her lungs for a long moment before releasing it. She lapsed into a coughing fit but was too tired and emotionally raw to care if she looked silly.

"Shit. That kind of crap happen much?" she asked.

"No. I mean, some gangs fight over their stupid tags and stuff, but serious crews aren't into that. GMan and his crew aren't legit. I hope Twist and the others are okay."

"Twist had an attitude, too."

"Guess he did." LadyP gave her a little grin. "So, *Mare*, that enough excitement for you? Ready to head back to the safety of art school?"

"I was just thinking about that. Come with me."

The grin disappeared. LadyP seemed to think that over. *Does she think I'm interested after all?*

"Not gonna happen. But I've been looking into some jobs here. Henry has been helping me."

"You're saying you'll stay off the streets now?"

"I think so." LadyP paused. "Damn, I'll miss it."

"Me too. But I'm going back to Savannah tomorrow."

TWELVE

ELAINE WASN'T PREPARED for the shock of returning to New York City after only three short months in Savannah. How could she have forgotten that two thousand people were murdered there last year? Crack cocaine, heroin, and AIDS now accounted for hundreds more deaths every year. And the dirt. Not just in the subway, even the city streets. The only redeeming factor, as she emerged from the subway, was the Christmas lights. Blinking bright red and green up and down the sidewalks, just like the song. Oh, and the snow! Savannah hadn't seen snow since 1977, and then only a couple of inches, so she wasn't likely to enjoy this scene when she went back to SCAD after the holidays. Christmas—especially the seventy-five foot Norway spruce at Rockefeller Center—did much to redeem the grittier aspects of the city.

She had flown into JFK and had taken the train straight to Union Station. Graffiti messages on the trains and the walls of the subway stations reminded her of Mare. She had to remind herself that the girl was only sixteen years old. *So much potential—if she would only start making some better choices.* She had reconsidered her emotional decision to quit teaching at SCAD and planned to return for the spring semester after the holidays.

Elaine wanted to get a taste of Manhattan before heading down to the Village. She looked forward to shopping at Bergdorf and Bloomingdale's, eating at the River Café and the Empire Diner. And listening to good music. Elaine loved jazz, and The Village was filled with it. She couldn't wait to meet up with old friends at some of their favorite haunts. After a few hours of window-shopping and café-sitting in Manhattan, she got back on the subway and headed to the Village to see Willem.

Walking the two blocks from the subway station to their apartment, Elaine was filled with a strange mix of nostalgia and fear. Their marriage had been anything but idyllic, and yet he had been the love of her life. Until the drinking got worse— which led to more affairs. Mostly one-night stands, but they still hurt. She had told him she would be arriving today, partly out of courtesy and partly to "warn" him in case he needed or wanted to make any changes in his sleeping arrangements before she got there.

Why do I even put up with his behavior? She considered this for the umpteenth time as she walked up the steps to their apartment. They didn't keep score, but her affairs had been as plentiful as his. Their marriage was as much a partnership between two artists—almost a business agreement—as it was a dysfunctional love affair. After all, he'd discovered her and catapulted her into the Ab Ex scene when she was previously unknown. And damned if she didn't still love him in spite of it all.

Her hand shook as she tried to put her key into the lock. After a couple of failed attempts—dropping her keys onto the icy stoop at one point—she was about to try again when she decided to give the knob a turn. Click ... it opened easily. Willem didn't even have the door locked, an old habit she would have thought he'd changed in light of the current wave of crime in the city.

"Willem?" she called out as she stepped inside. She turned around to pick up her suitcase and pull it into the foyer before yanking the door closed on the wintry weather. "It's me, Elaine. Are you here?"

No answer. She stepped around the staircase into the living room. No sign of Willem, but plenty of signs he had been there—newspapers littered the floor and coffee table. Empty liquor bottles were everywhere.

Elaine had listened to his excuses for years. Their similarly abusive childhoods had been part of the emotional glue that held them together through several decades of shitstorms. She knew all too well the stories of his childhood in working-class Rotterdam—divorced parents, beaten by his mother, becoming an apprentice at twelve and entering the city's Academy of Fine Arts at thirteen. He eventually stowed away on a freighter to New York, where he continued to live hand-to-mouth, working his way up in the art world until he became the most influential painter of the 1950s. To many people, Willem de Kooning embodied the romantic figure with movie-star good looks and a confident swagger. He spent many evenings at the Cedars Tavern in Greenwich Village with Jackson Pollock. His reputation as a womanizer was well known, but his often raucous depiction of women wasn't always praised by critics and art historians. By the 1970s his stellar reputation had greatly declined. And now—as 1983 was coming to a close—his career was in shambles.

On top of the drinking, dementia had begun to set in. More than ten years Elaine's senior, Willem's physical and mental decline were inevitable. And yet he continued to paint into his late seventies. Where would she find him today?

She followed the lingering smell of bacon and checked the kitchen—almost expecting to find an unattended burner forgotten on the stove—but found instead evidence of a meal he had shared with someone earlier in the day. Two placemats with dirty silverware and half-empty glasses were on the kitchen table. Two plates with scraps of eggs and bits of toast hanging onto them were stacked in the sink. Her anxiety heightened as she walked up the stairs to the bedroom they had shared in their on-again, off-again relationship. The door was closed. Should she knock, although it was still technically her bedroom?

Tapping gently, she again called out, "Bill? It's Elaine."

She heard a loud thump and didn't wait for an answer. Opening the door, she found Willem in a tangle of blankets on the floor, leaving a female body half covered by the bed sheets. The woman had reached for a nearby throw and was trying to slip away to the bathroom without attracting attention.

"No need to cover up on my account, honey. I was just leaving." She turned to walk out of the room, but Willem called after her.

"Please don't leave, Elaine. I guess I missed your call, but I'm glad you're here."

"I can see that." Elaine didn't turn around as she answered him, but continued out of the bedroom, down the stairs, and out the front door. Catching a taxi just outside the apartment, she could no longer hold back the tears. She thought she had prepared herself emotionally for a scene like this, but it always surprised her. And it hurt as much now as it ever had.

"Where to?" the driver asked, looking at Elaine in his rear-view mirror. "Hey, lady, are you okay?"

"Not yet, but I will be. Just take me to the Vanguard."

"Sure thing. Love the Vanguard—my cousin works the kitchen there. You know that new girl from Mississippi is singing there with the M-Base Collective tonight. Think her name is Cassandra Wilson."

Jazz. That was what she needed, and a stiff drink. She would also need time—to figure out her next move.

• • •

It was dark inside the club, but as Elaine was finding her way to a table she recognized Milton Resnick and his wife, Pat Paslof, fellow artists with whom she and Willem had been friends for many years—they had studios in two old abandoned synagogues on the Lower East Side. Milton rose and greeted Elaine warmly, with kisses on both cheeks. He was Russian.

"What on earth are you doing here, darling? I thought you were down South somewhere inspiring young artists."

He held a chair out for Elaine to join them. She exchanged kisses with Pat and sat down.

"First semester is over so I thought I'd spend Christmas here in New York."

"Darling, get her a drink." Pat nudged Milton as she turned her attention to Elaine. "Have you seen Bill yet?"

"Oh, my ... that's a conversation that *must* wait until that drink arrives." Elaine reached for her cigarettes and muffled a nervous laugh with a cough. "What's that concoction you're having, Pat?"

"It's a Kir. Crème de cassis and white wine. Very Christmassy, don't you think?"

Elaine eyed Milton's bourbon but opted to join Pat with the more festive choice. She needed a mood lifter. The music was helping.

"Who's that on the sax?"

"That's Steve Coleman." Milton nodded toward the stage. "The singer is from Mississippi—Cassandra something or other."

Elaine's drink arrived and she began to relax. Pat asked her about the teaching gig at SCAD, and Elaine answered with a few vague descriptions of the classes she was teaching. No mention of Mare—she just didn't want to go there. She finally told Pat and Milton about the state in which she found Willem earlier.

"Have you seen him while I've been gone? I mean, has he gotten worse—the drinking?"

Milton shrugged and Pat took another sip of her cocktail and watched the band.

"What aren't you telling me?" Elaine touched Pat on the arm.

Pat looked at Milton first, then said, "He doesn't get out much. And when he does, he always has a different young woman with him. Someone who can help pour him into a taxi and get him home safely."

"I'm sure those flings aren't serious," Milton offered.

"Oh, believe me, I know. And it's not as though I haven't had plenty myself. But it's his health I'm worried about—I can't just ignore him."

Before either Pat or Milton could respond, the band picked up the pace—the saxophonist, Greg Osby, let out a wailing solo, and the jazzy vibe filled the harried space in her head. Elaine lit another cigarette but began to cough almost violently after a couple of puffs. This wasn't good—the hacking had never been this bad.

"Are you all right?" Pat leaned in so Elaine could hear her above the music.

"Sure. Just this nagging smoker's cough."

Milton ordered bagels with lox and cream cheese and an assorted plate of antipasto. While they ate, they joined other patrons with outbursts of applause for Wilson's soulful crooning

and Osby's sax work, which ranged from powerful to tender—
just what Elaine's wounded heart needed during the Christmas
holidays. As the waitress brought their check, Milton asked if
they could give Elaine a lift home.

"Or, perhaps, to a hotel?" he added.

"Damn. I left my suitcase at the apartment. I really don't
want to stay there tonight. But that little tart was on her way
out, so I guess I might as well head back. I'd love a ride, thanks."

• • •

Minutes later Milton and Pat dropped Elaine at the apartment and she again climbed the stairs, this time with added
determination (and two cocktails) in her gut. She found Willem
in the kitchen. He was drinking coffee, probably trying to wash
the alcohol out of his system.

"I really am sorry." He tried the old smile, the one that usually
charmed Elaine no matter how offensive his actions.

"I know, Bill. It's not the girl, really. But you're going to kill
yourself with the booze if you don't get some help. There's a
clinic—"

"Already looked into it. Found a doctor to write me a prescription for Antabuse."

"But don't you need someone with you when you're taking
that?"

"You mean a policeman to be sure I don't drink? That's the
point, Elaine. The stuff makes you sick if you drink."

Elaine set her purse on the kitchen counter and remained
on her feet. "So what keeps you from skipping a pill in order
to drink? Seems like you need to be in a treatment center or
something."

"Got that covered. I've bought a small place on Long Island.
Moving there right after Christmas. Hired someone to be with
me for the first few weeks, at least."

"I see. And just when were you going to tell me this?" Elaine began pacing the floor. "What if I hadn't come to New York for Christmas? What if I'd come after spring semester? Would I have found some tenant in our apartment, asked where you were and had to listen to her say, 'I'm not sure. Upstate, maybe?'"

"I'm telling you now. I didn't want to call you at the school. Didn't want you to panic and quit teaching or anything."

Their eyes met. His were swollen, and his pale skin showed the years of alcohol abuse. She saw the same old broken-down Willem she'd dealt with for most of her life. She had tried to get him to take Antabuse before, and she wanted to believe he was ready now.

"What about the apartment? *Our* apartment?" She reached into her purse and pulled out a pack of cigarettes. She lit up, coughed some more, and looked around for an ashtray. Willem pointed to a shelf near the sink. She found one and brought it back to the table and sat down.

"You can keep it if you want to. But I thought you might want to come to Long Island when you get finished at Savannah. We could sublet it until then. You don't have to decide now."

Elaine gazed at him. Then she stubbed her cigarette and stood. "You know what? Just do whatever the *fuck* you want with the apartment, Bill. And I hope you can kick the sauce this time, but you'll have to do it without me."

"I understand. That's why I got someone to stay with me there, Elaine. I wasn't expecting you to quit your gig at SCAD," Willem replied, his voice cracking. He gave her a desperate smile, but she wasn't having it—she grabbed her purse and strode to the door to retrieve her suitcase. "Elaine, please ..."

She didn't look back as she walked out the door.

THIRTEEN

MARE'S DORM WAS mostly empty when she returned to Savannah from Atlanta. Only a couple of foreign students who couldn't make it home for the holidays were in the building. The emptiness was almost spooky. Mare jumped when she heard a knock on her door late in the afternoon on Christmas Eve.

"Who's there?" she called out from behind the locked door.

"It's Yuri. From down the hall."

Mare opened her door to find an Asian girl she had only seen in passing. "Oh, hi. I wasn't sure who else was in the building."

Yuri smiled. "I know. It's kinda weird, isn't it? A few of us were going out tonight. We found a restaurant that's serving until ten. Want to join us?"

Mare hadn't even thought about what to do on Christmas Eve. Or the next day, for that matter. It wasn't like she was missing her magical childhood filled with holiday treats and visits from Santa. She was just planning on spending the rest of the holidays working in the studio.

"Oh, thanks. But I'm okay. I picked up some food from a deli and I'm kinda tired. Thought I'd just watch some old movies or something."

"Cool. Let me know if you change your mind."

Mare watched the girl walk down the hall before closing her door. Opening a bag of chips and a soda, she settled onto her couch and reached for her piecebook. Images of work she had thrown up reminded her of a part of her life she was moving on from. And then there were other sketches she never brought to life on the street. But she was realizing she was okay with that. She closed the covers of the book—and that season of her life, hopefully—for good.

The truth was that the fight in Atlanta between the competing graf crews had really shaken her up. She thought of Elaine and wondered what she was doing in New York. Was she really spending Christmas Eve with Willem? How could she go back to him after the way she said he'd treated her over the years? Old people were so damned confusing. Would she be that messed up when she was Elaine's age?

· · ·

She spent Christmas day and several afterward in the studio. If she was going to be a serious artist, she knew she had to pour her passion into her classes. She still had a lot to learn, and it was a miracle she was even at SCAD at all. Even without Elaine there to mentor her this spring, she could learn from the other professors. Not to mention working hard in the studio—and staying off the streets.

She was walking across campus from the studio to her dorm later that week when she heard a familiar voice behind her on the sidewalk. "Mare! Wait up."

A confused expression was all Mare could muster as she turned around to find Elaine walking hurriedly toward her. "Elaine? What are you doing here? I thought you weren't coming back ..."

"I know that's what I said. But I was hoping—can we just talk?"

Mare nodded at a nearby bench and they walked over to it. Mare set down her backpack, then reached inside and pulled out a pack of cigarettes. She lit one and offered the pack to Elaine.

"What are you doing?" Elaine almost screamed at her. "Haven't you seen what smoking has done to me?"

Recovering from her surprise at seeing her professor, Mare put one hand on her hip and raised the cigarette to her mouth with the other hand. She didn't answer—just stared at Elaine, allowing a slight smirk to escape from her mouth.

"Answer me! What the *hell* are you doing with those cigarettes?"

"Yeah, and I'm sure no one ever tried to tell you to quit, right, Elaine? Or to quit getting drunk all the time like you did in the hotel when we were in Atlanta." Now Mare was pacing in front of her mentor and taking frequent drags. "And how can you preach at me when you screwed around with all those men? Oh, I know you've told me a million times that everybody in the art scene in New York was doing it—like that made it okay. You even made excuses for your husband's affairs. Did you sleep with him during the holidays in New York, like nothing was even wrong?" Mare came to a stop, cigarette burning, and glared at Elaine, daring her to respond.

"I haven't had an affair in years!" Elaine yelled back. "And no, I didn't sleep with him in New York!" She looked away briefly and pursed her mouth. "If you must know, he was with someone else when I got to his apartment. Not that it's any of your business."

"You make it my business when you lecture me, Elaine. How do you expect me to respect you and learn from you when your personal life is such a train wreck?"

Mare watched Elaine's face for signs of hurt. She wanted her to feel some pain, but she didn't want to close the door completely. As she thought about their relationship and where it might be headed, Yuri and another girl walked down the sidewalk nearby. Yuri waved at Mare, and Mare returned the gesture with a nod and a quick smile.

"So, you still want me to teach you?" Elaine stomped out her cigarette and looked Mare in the face.

"I don't know. Are you finished with Willem?"

Elaine drew a tired breath and explained about Willem's decision to get treatment for his alcoholism, and about the house on Long Island.

"So now you're going to go take care of him, right? Men shit all over us and expect us to just take it."

"You're not old enough to understand this yet, but when you've loved someone for as many years as Willem and I have shared, you learn to forgive. We shared a lifetime together. And I wouldn't be the artist I am today without him."

"Yeah. That's what I figured." Mare picked her up backpack and started to walk away when Elaine grabbed her arm to stop her.

"Wait. I'm not moving back there. He hired a caregiver. I told him I was coming back to SCAD. I'm here for you if you'll have me." Tears filled Elaine's eyes. "I believe in you. Please let me help you."

Screw this. Now you're going all sweet on me. Without looking up at Elaine, she said, "Okay."

"Just *okay*? That's it?" Elaine held both hands up, then let them fall to her sides. "I'm willing to make a commitment to you, Mare, but I need the same from you."

Mare kicked at the ground. When she found her voice, the hard edge was gone. "I need to tell you something. Maybe we should sit down."

Elaine gave her a long look. Then they both sat. Mare stubbed her cigarette, lit another one, and again offered the pack to Elaine. Elaine hesitated, then took one. Mare lit it for her.

"I did go to Atlanta," she began, looking off into the distance. "But I went to find a couple of graffiti writers I met when we went to the art gallery. Couldn't find them but a waitress at a café told me how to get to a shelter. When I got there I found LadyP—one of the writers I met before."

Mare waited for Elaine to sigh, or curse, or something—but she didn't say a word.

"Maybe I needed one last go-round, to get it out of my system. As soon as LadyP said she was with some new crew that was going out, I said 'I'm in.' It was a bunch of guys—they didn't want LadyP and me helping—and they were painting over this throw-up this rival group had done, saying how those dudes were stealing their work. All of a sudden this other group of boys comes running up, and it's that very crew and punches are being thrown and I got hit in the head and knocked down. LadyP and I got out of there, got back to the shelter in one piece, and the guy who runs the shelter got me some ice to put on the knot on my head."

Now Mare felt the stirrings of tears. She blinked them back and faced Elaine, who still hadn't said a word.

"I was sitting there with LadyP thinking, 'What the *hell* am I doing here?' I told her I was going back to Savannah the next morning, which I did. I've been in the studio every day since— that's where I was coming from just now." She paused, trying for the right words. "I guess I wasn't ready last time we talked. But I am now. I won't let you down, Elaine. I swear I won't."

PART THREE

FOURTEEN

As **THE NEW** semester began, Mare's paintings became less dark, and her brush strokes were more controlled. Her style was changing—there was a folk art feel to some of her scenes—quite a departure from her original images, and certainly very different from her graffiti pieces. One day in the studio Mare stayed late after the other students left. Elaine found her painting a desert scene of two figures facing each other: a man wearing a priestly robe and a woman barely covered by a tattered cloth. They were both on their knees, as if in prayer.

"What's this?"

"It's a scene from the desert."

"Yes, I can see that. Who are those people?"

"That's the priest, Zosimas, and Mary of Egypt."

"You are obsessed with that story, aren't you?"

Mare wondered if she should tell Elaine how strong her feelings were about this Mary of Egypt person. *Will she laugh at me?* Even if Elaine didn't understand, Mare felt the need to tell her what a big deal it was to her.

"I just want to know more about them—the woman in the icon and the priest who found her in the desert. And ... you said you would help me, right? Well, this is what matters to me right now."

Having opened up, Mare braced herself ... and Elaine gave her a sweet smile.

"Well, I have a surprise for you. There's going to be a Tavener opera at the Wells Theatre this weekend. I've got two tickets. Would you like to go with me?"

"I've never really liked opera—who's Tavener? What's it about?"

Elaine smiled again and paused before answering. "The English National Opera commissioned John Tavener to write an opera about the life of Mary of Egypt."

"No way! That's amazing! When is it?"

"Eight o'clock Saturday night. I'll pick you up at seven."

As she rode her bicycle back to her dorm after class, Mare tried to imagine the story on her canvas set to music. She noticed a group of students sitting under the trees at one of the many scenic parks in the city. There was a nice breeze and the sun danced through the branches like nature's strobe lights. She stopped to catch her breath and listen to Bonnie Tyler singing "Holdin' Out For a Hero" on a jam box sitting on the grass. The disco beat almost drowned out the words but they found their way to her ears—she, too, wondered where all the good men had gone. Just then she noticed Flannery waving at her from the other side of the group of students. She dropped her bike and walked over and noticed a cute, sandy-haired boy with his arm around Flannery. She didn't recognize the boy, who was really a man, probably in his late twenties.

"Hi, Mare. This is Sean."

"Hey, nice to meet you." Mare gave Flannery a look that said *where have you been keeping this guy?*

"You, too. Want to join us?" Sean asked. He and Flannery scooted over, making room on the large blanket they had spread on the grass.

"Guess so." Mare sat down. "Where were you today, Flan? Didn't see you in studio."

"Yeah, I just needed a break. And Sean is only in town for a couple more days."

"Oh? Where did y'all meet?"

"At a concert last weekend. Sean's a roadie for Depeche Mode's U.S. tour. Hey, you wanna join us for their last gig this Saturday night? A bunch of us are going out after."

Mare never hung out with other students. And she had shunned the boys who were brave enough to try to talk with her. The last thing she wanted to do was tell Flannery about her plans to go to the opera with Elaine.

"Thanks, but I've got plans." And before they could ask, she quickly got up and headed back to her bike. She looked over her shoulder to wave goodbye but Flannery and Sean were already making out on their blanket as though she had never been there. As she rode away, she heard Marvin Gaye croon about sexual healing. Fitting, she thought.

• • •

As they entered the Wells Theatre on Saturday night, Mare and Elaine were greeted by materials, textures, and geometric angles that were part of its Art Moderne splendor. Intricate rectangular carvings repeated themselves along the walls. Gold leaf flickered off every surface. Even the curtain on the massive stage was itself a work of art—tapestries of shimmering gold and copper. The theater seated over a thousand patrons and boasted a state-of-the-art audio system. Just listening to the orchestra warming up sent chills down Mare's spine. The music wasn't familiar—it had a foreign, Middle Eastern sound—but even the concordant notes the musicians struck as they tuned their instruments simultaneously had an otherworldly beauty.

"Wow." Mare had never seen anything like this before.

Elaine smiled. An usher handed them each a program and showed them to their seats. The cover of the program featured an icon of Mary of Egypt and Zosimas. They quickly read the Composer's Note before the overture began, which was penned by John Tavener.

> *Mary's door was wide open, even though her love was misdirected and distorted ...*

They looked at each other, and then continued to read the rest of the program notes. Mare wondered how the words were hitting Elaine. She remembered how uncomfortable Elaine had been when they visited the Coptic church. *What's she thinking now?*

> *Zosimas's whole sound world becomes Mary's. In her he sees 'love' and his own limitations. His world, once so dry, now in the dryness of the desert, flowers into what the Desert Fathers might have called "Uncreated Eros" or a hint of the Edenic state. In controlled ecstasy, they both ask each other to give the blessing.*

"That's what's happening in your painting, isn't it?" Elaine whispered.

Mare nodded and they continued reading Taverner's comments:

> *"Mary of Egypt" is the intent to create an ikon in sound about Non-Judgement. In a sense, Zosimas loves again when through Mary he can dimly see the beauty of God—and who knows how far Mary has gone in her search for the unknowable and unobtainable in her forty solitary years in the desert? Holy Mary, pray to God for us.*

The orchestra finished warming up and the lights dimmed. A group of women and men formed two parallel lines on the stage, representing the extensions of Mary and Zosimas. The women's sensual movements were accompanied by a flute, wordlessly representing Mary whoring in Alexandria. The men were accompanied by the trombone and the primordial sound of the simantron—a wooden percussion instrument used in liturgical music (especially at monasteries) and sometimes with contemporary classical pieces. Each act was more powerful than the previous, building to a climax with the aria, "Bless." The characters of Zosimas and Mary—without their extensions from early scenes—prostrated themselves on the ground in front of each other, crying out in song the solitary word, "Bless!" over and over.

Mare wasn't prepared for how this would hit her—seeing the story she was growing more fascinated with by the day brought to life in such a powerful way on the stage. She felt some of the anger she'd hung onto over the years melt away as the words and music worked to soften her heart. *Damn.* She quickly brushed away tears, hoping Elaine hadn't seen them. Sneaking a glance at Elaine, Mare saw that she wasn't the only one weeping.

Then Mary levitated. The angels lifted her up—with help

from nearly invisible wires hung from the stage ceiling—leaving a terrified and awestruck Zosimas to grieve her loss. The opera continued with the conclusion of their story: Zosimas found Mary dead in the desert a year later and buried her with help from a lion, who appeared tame in the presence of the saint's remains.

Leaving the opera, Elaine reached for Mare's hand. "You need to go to that monastery."

Elaine's touch felt good—like a sweet aunt or a grandmother—someone she could trust. It was a new feeling for Mare, and she didn't pull her hand away.

"Oh, I'm so glad you understand. There's a workshop in the spring that hasn't filled yet. I think it's during spring break so I wouldn't miss class."

"I don't think that even matters at this point, Mare. You need to do this. We'll have plenty of time for class when you get back."

"Thank you, Elaine." She gripped her mentor's hand tightly before letting go, her mind already racing ahead as she began to imagine visiting the monastery and learning to write icons.

FIFTEEN

THE SIX-HOUR BUS ride on the first day of spring break offered Mare the chance to think about what she was doing. The trip brought up images of her escape from Forsyth to Macon last year. Hard to believe it was only a few months ago—it seemed like ages, and she felt so much older now. Those same feelings of fear and uncertainty returned at times during the day's trip, but it helped that she wasn't traveling at night. The view from her window revealed the colors of early spring—flowering trillium, wild ginger, mountain laurel—they all seemed to welcome her as she left behind the hustle and bustle of campus life and traveled deep into the woods of North Carolina.

A middle-aged woman in an ankle-length black skirt and

a long-sleeve blouse greeted Mare at the bus station in North Carolina. The small, rural town wasn't much more than a whistle stop, with only a few buildings nearby. The woman's hair was pulled back in a bandana. A smile was her only adornment.

"Hi. I'm Anna," she said. "I run errands for the nuns at the monastery. I'm parked over here." She offered to help Mare with her bag and led the way to a nearby van. "This your first time to take an icon workshop?"

"Yeah, um—yes ma'am."

Anna laughed. "I can tell you were raised in the South. There's no need to call me ma'am."

Mare blushed, remembering how she felt on her first day at SCAD when she was late for Elaine's studio class and fumbled with the rules of etiquette. If Anna was any indication, the monastery would introduce her to another new world. Mare hesitated before getting into the car.

"Okay if I have a smoke first? It's been a long trip."

"I guess so," Anna said, sounding surprised. "I mean, not in my car, but I'll wait for you if you want to smoke over there by that bench before we leave."

"Cool." Mare started for the bench. Anna followed.

"You know," she began slowly, "the nuns really don't like people to smoke at the monastery. But you can always walk down the gravel driveway to the entrance and smoke out by the road."

What have I gotten myself into? "Is it a sin or something?"

"Oh, no." Anna tucked a loose hair behind her bandana and straightened her skirt. Now she sounded almost embarrassed. "Nothing like that. It's just that most of the people who come don't smoke. Guess it's a health thing more than a religious thing."

"No problem," Mare said, knowing not to be rude. She finished the cigarette, stubbed it in the parking lot, and followed

Anna back to her car. Anna spoke again after pulling away from the bus station.

"So, are you Orthodox?"

"No."

"Then how did you get interested in iconography?"

"I saw icons at a Catholic church in Macon, Georgia. I used to live there. And then, well, I'm an art student now. One of my professors has kind of helped me learn more about them."

"Huh. Not many art students come to these workshops. Usually it's Orthodox people—or maybe Catholics—who are into icons."

"Well, I did see some beautiful Coptic icons at an Orthodox church in Atlanta. The priest there was super nice. He told me more stuff about them. He's the one who told me about the icon workshop."

"Ah, so you were sent here by Father Mark."

Mare looked at Anna. "You know him?"

"He comes to the monastery for our Feast Day every year. He'll be here in a few days—for the weekend. A lot of Coptic Orthodox priests visit St. Mary from time to time."

As they continued the drive through the snow-capped Blue Ridge Mountains, Mare's stomach began to growl. She was embarrassed, but Anna laughed.

"Forgive me. I should have asked if you were hungry after the long bus ride. There's a little café up ahead. Would you like to stop for some coffee or something to eat?"

"That would be great."

The trees were already taking on new foliage. May-apples, buttercups and Indian paintbrushes dotted the ever-changing landscape as they followed the curving highway. Craggy gardens appeared around every turn. The scene took Mare's breath away. They pulled into a little roadside mom-and-pop grocery and café. As they sat down in a booth by a large window, an older woman in a peasant blouse, long skirt, and apron took their orders. Mare stared out the window.

"It's—it's beautiful here."

"Yes, especially in spring when the snow begins to melt," Anna replied. "Everything just brims with new birth. The nuns get excited about Pascha right around this time every year."

"*Pascha?*"

"It's what you know as Easter. Did you grow up Protestant?"

"Not really. I'm not sure what you'd call it. My father started this place in Georgia called Heaven's Gate. A commune, sort of. We had our own church. That's where I lived until I was twelve."

Anna gave Mare a long look and then returned her attention to her coffee.

"You've heard of it?" Now Mare wished she hadn't mentioned the farm.

"Yes. Lots of groups spring up like that. People are looking for community—something akin to what the early Christians shared. But they're often misled—"

She bit the cuticles off the nails of her right hand as Anna's words hit her in the gut. *Misled? That what happened to my mom and the others at the farm? Was everybody there just stupid, or was my dad some sort of pied piper?*

"—oh, I'm sorry, Mare. Did you lose your family there?"

"All but my mother. She and I escaped when I was twelve. I haven't seen her since."

"That must have been hard. You know, some of the nuns at the monastery came here because they lost family members. Or suffered abuse. Or both, sometimes."

"How many nuns live here?" Mare asked. She was glad for the conversation to turn away from her own story.

"About a dozen right now. And one priest-monk, Father Zossima."

"Zossima?"

"Yeah—have you heard of him?"

"No, I mean, not *this* Zossima. The one in the story about Mary of Egypt."

"Yes. You know she's the patron saint of the monastery?"

Wait, did Father Mark tell me that? Seems like that woman is everywhere. "Whoa. I didn't realize ..."

"Father Zossima converted to Orthodoxy, like some of the nuns. But some are cradle Coptics."

"Cradle ...?"

Anna smiled. "They were born into the Orthodox Church, rather than converting later in life."

"Wow. That's a lot of new words to learn. Is there anything else I need to know—how to act, what to say—stuff like that?"

"Well, yes, actually. There's a brochure in the guesthouse. It explains about dressing respectfully and being quiet at the monastery. A schedule of church services is posted there, too."

"Okay ... I've noticed people at the Catholic Church in Macon and the Orthodox Church in Atlanta making certain gestures. Like bowing and kissing things—even the priest's hand. What's all that about?"

"Just signs of respect. When you meet a priest, you put one hand on top of the other—palms up—bow your head and say, 'Father, bless.' He will make the sign of the cross and place his hand on top of yours. You kiss his hand. That's how you receive his blessing. The nuns at the monastery also ask the blessing from the abbess in this way."

Mare hesitated. "Will I be expected to do that?"

"It's up to you, really. The nuns don't want visitors to be uncomfortable."

"What about kissing icons? I saw someone do that in Atlanta."

"Yes, that's also a sign of respect. You make the sign of the cross two times, make a bow—it's called a metania—then kiss the icon, then make the sign of the cross a third time."

"That's a lot to remember."

Anna laughed. "Don't worry. Just cross yourself once and kiss the icon if you want to. That's enough."

· · ·

Returning to the road after eating, Mare was lost in thoughts of kissing priests' hands and icons when they passed a battered sign by a gravel road off the highway that read SAINT AGNES HOME FOR GIRLS. Its paint was faded and the letters were barely legible.

"What's that place?" Mare pointed to the sign as they passed by.

"Used to be an orphanage. It's been closed for years. Evidently some Catholic nuns were accused of abusing the girls, back in the '40s and '50s. Even a priest."

Oh, God. That's when Elaine came to Black Mountain and left her baby in an orphanage ... Elaine and her daughter ... the baby girl at St. Agnes ... abused.

Even though Anna had said she didn't want smoking in the car, Mare lit a cigarette, cracked the window, and was silent for the rest of the drive. Anna didn't say anything, and if she sensed anything was wrong, she didn't speak up. Soon they pulled into a gravel parking lot. Anna pointed to a building on their right. "That's the monastery guesthouse. I'll help you with your bag."

Mare was immediately struck by the beauty of the grounds, which lightened her mood a bit after the heartbreaking connection she'd made on the highway. The flowerbeds were meticulously manicured and filled with colorful flora, even in March. Flowering Cherry, forsythia, Star Magnolia, and Carolina jessamine filled the spaces between the shrubs. Periwinkle, violets, crocus, daffodils, hyacinths, and tulips lined the neatly-swept sidewalks. The sidewalks connected several buildings, which faced each other in a square.

CHERRY BOMB

"Most of the buildings were made with reclaimed barn lumber, giving them a historic presence, although they were built in the last ten years," Anna said, now standing next to Mare. "That's the refectory—the dining room—right next to the chapel. Over there."

Mare looked up to see the sun sinking behind the chapel. It cast an aura around the domed cupola like a halo around the head of a saint.

"Oh, wow," she whispered. "Man, that's beautiful."

Anna led Mare into the guesthouse and past a common area where several people were sitting in chairs—some were reading, others chatting quietly. A few steps beyond the lobby they entered a small room with a single bed, bureau, bedside table, desk, and chair. A towel and washcloth were on the foot of the bed, along with a neatly-folded, rust-colored blanket. A small hooked rug only covered a small area of the wide-plank pine floor. An icon of a woman receiving communion from a priest hung above the bed. Mare recognized Saint Mary of Egypt and the priest Zossima. The room was about the same size as the one at the homeless shelter, but this one was neat and clean—almost cheerful. Mare was suddenly filled with memories of the events just a few months ago. She wondered what LadyP was doing now, and what LadyP would think of her being at a monastery.

"This is your room, Mare. The bathrooms are down the hall. You might want to freshen up and change clothes before the evening church service. It begins in about fifteen minutes."

"But it's optional, right?"

Anna smiled. "Of course. But you might not want to miss this one. This is the fifth week of Great Lent. Tonight they read *The Life of Saint Mary of Egypt*. They always bring in a miracle-working icon from a nearby cathedral for the week. This coming Sunday is actually the Sunday of Mary of Egypt."

"Oh—is that the weeping icon Father Mark told me about?"

"Yes, it's been weeping for about three years, I think."

Since I was thirteen ... one year after Mother and I escaped from the farm and she left me in Macon. Mare barely heard Anna's voice as she explained about the icon.

"You can see tears coming out of her eyes—like a fragrant oil. People anoint themselves with it and pray for healing."

"Uh ... who painted it—the weeping icon?"

"I don't really know. The rumor goes that an abused woman did the icon, and the nuns took it to a cathedral so that a bishop could verify its authenticity. It stays at the cathedral now, except on certain feast days when they bring it here to the monastery church."

"Do they know why the icon weeps?" Mare asked.

"The abbess here at the monastery says that Saint Mary herself has been weeping in Heaven for all the women and children who have been abused or abandoned. Some people think Saint Mary was abused as a child. But no one really knows. Lots of people come to see the icon and to ask for the saint's prayers." Anna paused and smiled again. "Well, make yourself comfortable. The workshop starts tomorrow morning at nine. There's a schedule of church services on the back of the door here."

"Thank you, Anna. For everything."

• • •

Mare wished it was already tomorrow morning and she was sitting in the icon workshop, beginning to learn iconography. She would be comfortable there—in a studio setting—doing art. Tonight her thoughts were painful. She unpacked her things into the small bureau and changed into a skirt and blouse she'd found in a Savannah thrift shop. Her hands shook as she tied a scarf around her hair. She was craving a smoke but knew there wasn't time to dash down to the road before the service began. Catching a glimpse of herself in the mirror, she wondered who the hell *that* girl was. She darted from the guesthouse at the sound of the bells tolling the evening vigil and the evocative tones of the talanton—the long wooden bar and mallet used to summon the nuns to church the way Noah called the animals to the ark. She remembered reading about the talanton in Sir John Taverner's notes from the opera program and thought of Elaine for a second.

The sound stirred something in her heart:

To TAL an ton to TAL an ton to TA to TA to TAL an ton.

She hurried into the darkened chapel, nearly tripping over the curled edge of a worn, knotted pile rug. As her eyes adjusted to the candlelight, she noticed an icon on a stand in the middle of the nave. A candle stand beside it was full of shimmering tapers. She found an empty chair among the other visitors and started to sit down, but everyone was standing. An older woman next to her whispered, "That's the weeping icon of Saint Mary of Egypt. Do you want to put a candle there and ask her prayers?"

Mare looked closer at the icon and saw how much it looked like those in the churches in Macon and Atlanta—the same semi-naked image of a woman with sunbaked skin and long white hair. But this icon had a clear acrylic container attached to its base. The container appeared to be filling with a liquid, which dripped slowly from the icon.

"What is that—in the container?" Mare asked the woman.

"Her tears. It's a miracle. They say she's weeping sweet myrrh. Go ahead. Venerate it—here, I'll show you."

Before Mare could object, the woman took her by the arm and they moved closer to the icon. The woman crossed herself and kissed the icon on Saint Mary's right hand. Then she stepped aside and nodded at Mare, handing her a candle.

"Light it from one of the other tapers and place it in the sand. Saint Mary will pray for you."

Mare's hand was shaking. She lit the candle from the flames

and placed it among the others, increasing their brilliance by one. Then she followed the woman back to their seats. Nuns in black habits were now assembled along the far side of the nave: three at the readers' stand, the rest in various states of prostration—some on their knees and curled into little black balls, their faces to the ground, hands tucked under their foreheads. No flesh was visible, no sign of their womanhood. Mare adjusted her own head covering, tucking strands of hair under the edges of the scarf. Her fingers tugged clumsily at the fabric, pulling it over her ears.

The scene could have been playing out in ancient Romania or Greece or Russia. But this was 1984, Mare thought, and she was in an Orthodox monastery in the mountains of North Carolina. How surreal! Her eyes searched the faces of the sisters as they rose from their prostrations to sing the evening hymns. The sun made its final appearance of the day, shooting polygons of light through the amber panes of the narrow, deep-set windows in the chapel and illumining the gold leaf halos of the icons and the faces of the nuns. Even their ears and the lower parts of their chins were covered by the black habits, so that only inverted triangles of flesh were visible, like white theatrical masks. No traces of makeup smoothed the blemishes of the young or the wrinkles of the old.

Yet Mare saw a subtle, clear-eyed beauty that emanated from each one. No colorful gloss plumped their lips, which appeared small and turned in on themselves. They were like the mouths painted on the icons that filled the walls of the chapel, quivering on the verge of Mona Lisa smiles as though they had just tasted something delicious or were trying to keep a secret.

And then there was this whole business of kissing things. Icons. Crosses. Relics. Even the hands of the abbess and the priest. The visitors' instructions in the guesthouse were pretty clear: *No lipstick, please. No bare arms, legs, or feet.* Mare tugged at the sleeves of her blouse, tucked her bare, sandal-clad feet under her chair (were they serious about the sock rule?) and closed her eyes. Breathing in the otherworldly aroma of the incense and the oil burning in the lampadas, she hushed the voices in her head and was left with the sound of silence. She could hear her heart beating, physically, in her chest. And then another voice cut through the rarified atmosphere, a voice at once familiar and strange, full of depth and quiet confidence. And reverence. One of the nuns had begun to read.

"The Life of our Holy Mother Mary of Egypt. Mother, bless the reading."

The nun bowed toward the abbess, who made the sign of the cross above her head and offered her hand for a kiss.

"*It is good to hide the secret of a king, but it is glorious to reveal and preach the works of God.* So said the Archangel Raphael to Tobit when he performed the wonderful healing of his blindness. Actually, not to keep the secret of a king is perilous and a terrible risk, but to be silent about the works of God is a great loss for the soul. And I—says Saint Sophronius, in writing the life of Saint Mary of Egypt—am afraid to hide the works of God by silence ..."

Mare temporarily forgot herself as the words floated across the room, borne on their passage, it seemed, by mystical forces. It was the same story Father Mark had told her in Atlanta, but it seemed much more vivid tonight when read as part of a church service. The discomfort with her clothing—her wayward hair escaping the scarf, the nakedness of her toes—fell away from the edges of her consciousness, clearing her mental palette for new colors, preparing the canvas of her heart for new images. Her senses were aroused by the incense, the candlelight on egg tempera icons, the talantons, the bells, and now ... that voice.

Where have I heard that voice before?

As the nun continued to read the story of Mary of Egypt,

Mare listened with rapt attention to the graphic details—many of which Father Mark had left out of Mary's wanton life in Egypt, where she lived as a prostitute.

"Every abuse of nature I regarded as life." The nun read these words and others that described her depravity. As she read, several of the nuns made prostrations, crossing themselves and weeping quietly. Even some visitors were moved to tears by the story. Especially the part where Mary was finally allowed to enter the church to venerate the true cross and, at the end, when the lion licked Mary's feet and helped Zossima bury her.

The nun finished the reading. All the others stood and sang hymns to this woman, Mary of Egypt, who was canonized by the Church for her repentance and her ascetic struggles and the miracles she wrought.

> *Having been a sinful woman,*
> *You became through repentance a Bride of Christ.*
> *Having attained angelic life,*
> *You defeated demons with the weapon of the Cross.*
> *Therefore, most glorious Mary, You are a Bride of*
> *   the Kingdom!*
> *Therefore your spirit, Holy Mother Mary, rejoices*
> *   with the angels!*

Afterward, the abbess led the nuns in venerating the weeping icon. Father Zossima stood beside it holding a small brush, which he dipped in the "tears" as they streamed into the container. Then he anointed each worshipper by making the sign of the cross on their foreheads and on the backs and the palms of their hands saying, "For the healing of soul and body."

When the woman next to Mare nudged her to go forward for the anointing, Mare whispered, "But what if I don't believe? I'm not Orthodox—I'm here to take an icon class. And even if God does exist, well, I'm pretty mad at Him right now."

The woman smiled. "God knows." And she gave Mare another gentle nudge.

As Mare approached the icon she thought she smelled roses, but she hadn't seen any roses in the chapel. Father Zossima smiled as he touched the brush to her forehead and made two short strokes, one vertical and one horizontal. She wanted to run, but she couldn't move.

Father Zossima leaned forward and spoke softly. "Your hands, please?"

Mare offered her hands, palms down and then palms up, as she had seen the others before her do. She watched, as if in a trance, while Father Zossima anointed them with the fragrant oil. She breathed in the aroma. Another drop of oil fell into the container.

It was the last thing Mare remembered before she hit the floor.

• • •

When she woke up in her room in the guesthouse, a pretty young nun was sitting beside her bed.

"I'm Sister Martha. You're going to be fine. You fainted."

"The oil." Mare smelled her hands. "It's real, isn't it? I mean, it's really coming from the icon. I thought maybe it was a trick, but I saw it. I smelled it."

The nun smiled. "Yes, it's a pretty powerful experience, isn't it? Your first time?"

"I've seen icons—this same Mary of Egypt person—but they didn't have oil dripping out of them. Did I cause a scene back in the chapel? I don't even remember fainting."

"The woman standing next to you helped you."

Mare sat up and swung her legs off the side of the bed.

"Be careful. Are you dizzy?"

"No, I'm fine. Actually, I'm a little hungry." *And I'd love a smoke, but probably not the best time.*

"That's a good sign. Mother Christina is waiting for you in the refectory. She asked me to bring you to her when you awoke."

"Mother Christina?" Mare asked.

"Oh, yes. She's the abbess—she's in charge of the nuns here."

Mare followed Sister Martha to the refectory, where Mother Christina greeted her with a plate of fresh fruit and homemade bread with peanut butter and jam. The room was large and the walls were covered with murals. The paintings all contained figures with halos, which seemed to tell stories. One showed a woman with a flask, kneeling beside another woman who appeared to be sick or injured.

"That's Saint Brigid. She lived in Ireland in the fifth century," Mother Christina said. Her voice was pleasant. She appeared to be around forty, but her skin had a timeless beauty and her eyes—an unusual green—seemed to reflect a light from within. "Saint Brigid was known for her care of the sick and the poor."

Mare scanned the walls, stopping at a large image of two women. One was obviously Mary of Egypt. The other was a woman holding a bowl with flames coming from it.

"I recognize Saint Mary," Mare said, "but who's beside her? What's the fire all about?"

"You are right about Saint Mary—she is the patron of our monastery. And although she and Brigid never met, our nuns wanted this painting to show their partnership in the faith. Mary represents repentance and the ascetic struggle. Brigid reminds us of our responsibility to serve our fellow man."

"And the flame?"

"That's perpetual fire, representing wisdom, poetry, healing, therapy, metallurgy, the hearth. We value the arts here at Saint Mary. That's why we offer the iconography classes. We also sponsor writing workshops. And speakers from the healing arts."

They stood quietly for a moment. Then Mother Christina said, "Would you care for a cup of tea?"

"Yes, thank you." Mare found a chair at the table and the abbess sat across from her and poured their tea.

"The sisters tell me that you are here to take an icon class. A student at SCAD, right?"

"My interests are abstract expressionism and primitive art. I guess that led me to icons—especially the Coptic style. Elaine—Elaine de Kooning; she's one of my professors—took me to Atlanta to see the icons at a Coptic church there."

"That's where you met Father Mark?"

Mare nodded and sipped her tea. It was scary putting herself out there to these people—especially since they were religious, like her father. But these nuns—and Father Mark—had a kindness about them that invited trust. And if she was done with her life on the street, she had to trust someone.

"He will be here this weekend," Mother Christina replied. "To celebrate the Sunday of Saint Mary of Egypt."

"She gets a Sunday in her name?"

"Yes. The fifth Sunday of Great Lent. She is the foremost example of repentance for Orthodox Christians. So, are you excited about the workshop?"

Mare nodded, then began to devour the homemade bread and scuppernong jam. Mother Christina smiled.

"You must be exhausted from your trip and then your experience with the icon tonight. I'll walk you back to the guesthouse. You need some sleep, I know."

"Mother ... uh, is that what I should call you ...?"

The smile broadened. "Yes, that will be fine."

"Can I ask you something first?"

"Of course."

"The nun who read Mary's story tonight—who is she?"

"Her name is Sister Susannah."

"Something's familiar about her voice. Where is she from?"

Mother Christina folded her hands and looked at Mare as she finished her tea. She considered her answer before she spoke.

"When women come to the monastery, they leave their life in the world behind," she said. "Some prefer never to speak of it—especially if they've been deeply wounded, or if they have hurt others in an unforgivable way. They come to repent. To seek healing. Sometimes isolation helps. Sister Susannah never interacts with visitors. She primarily helps with church services. And she is a beautiful painter. She does icon commissions to raise money for the monastery."

"She paints? *Icons?*"

"Yes. When she first came here she showed an interest in art. One of the older nuns trained her in iconography. She works alone most of the time."

"Can I see her work? Can I meet her?"

"Probably not, Mare. She needs her solitude. And you'll be busy enough with the workshop this week. Sister Gabriella will be your teacher."

The moon was almost full as they walked back to the guest-house. As anxious as Mare was for the workshop to begin, she couldn't quit thinking about Sister Susannah. Mother Christina must have sensed her uneasiness and gave her a gentle hug at the door to the guesthouse.

"I'm glad you're here, Mare. The workshop starts at nine. Please join us for prayers in the chapel first, though. We begin at five."

"*Five?* In the *morning?*"

Mother Christina laughed. "Yes. That's what we do here, Mare. We pray."

The abbess said goodnight and walked away. Alone now with her memories of childhood, Mare's heart was racing. The icon of Mary of Egypt hovered above her bed, which she gazed at while thinking about Mary possibly being abused as a child ... and Elaine leaving her child at a place just down the road long ago. Images of her father's hands on her in the "chapel" on the farm flashed through her head, followed by Uncle Miles' filthy body defiling her. She took a deep breath and squeezed her eyes shut, trying to clear her head. Then she grabbed her cigarettes and lighter from her purse.

"Damn right I'll go outside and smoke," she murmured as she crept down the hall. "Especially if they expect me to get up at five in the damn morning and pray."

SIXTEEN

THE CAMPUS EMPTIED quickly for spring break, leaving Elaine to the peace and quiet of a week of solitude. Well, at least it was quiet. Her mind was anything but peaceful. She couldn't quit thinking about that summer at Black Mountain, especially knowing that Mare would be spending a week in the area.

Late on Friday afternoon she unlocked a cabinet behind the desk in her office and pulled out several canvases rolled up together and tied with string. Mare had caught her looking at them that day she told her about Lily. It marked the first time she had told anyone about her daughter. No one knew except the long-forgotten folks in North Carolina at the time of her birth and those she met when she left Lily at the orphanage.

Perhaps it was time to face down the demons of her past so she could move forward.

Elaine took a deep breath and opened another cabinet. She pulled out a glass and a bottle of Jack Daniels—reinforcements. But the whiskey burned just enough to remind her of the pain.

The first painting showed a baby's head coming out of what appeared to be a giant lily. Two petals, white and smooth. They were open wide, as though giving birth to the child. Elaine touched the petals, running her finger along the raised edges of the paint. She had used a palette knife to give the petals fullness, like a woman's vulva during labor. The baby's face was pink; the eyes were tiny black dots and the mouth a bright red oval. More colorful than some of her abstracts, more vibrant. Penciled in at the bottom was LILY—1948.

Elaine closed her eyes and let herself remember.

• • •

"I'm going to North Carolina for a year."

There was silence on the other end of the call, then Willem's voice. "North Carolina? Who the hell's in North Carolina?"

Willem was in Maine, painting and holding court with a bevy of Ab Ex groupies.

"It's an artist colony, Bill. Like where you are. I need to get out of Manhattan."

"Who's going to watch the studio?"

"I can sublet it. Anyway, wanted to let you know. I'm leaving in a week."

"Who is he, Elaine?"

She considered telling him, just for a moment. She chose to be vague instead.

"It's my career, Bill. Can't you just accept that? I'll call when I get settled in."

It was her first time to really assert herself since they had gotten married. She had put up with his travels and his affairs. He could think what he wanted.

After arranging for some starving artists to sublet the studio, she packed her '41 Austin and headed for North Carolina, thankful for her car's efficiency (gasoline was only sixteen cents a gallon). The car was small, but large enough to hold her paint supplies and new clothes—a couple of sizes larger than her usual wardrobe. It would be easy enough to hide her condition with an artist's smock. She knew that eventually the truth must be revealed, but all she could think about now was having the freedom to explore her art without Willem and all of New York City looking over her shoulder.

The twelve-hour drive passed quickly, with only her bladder pressing her to stop along the way. It was tempting to spend some time in D.C., but her mission propelled her to keep moving.

She had not been prepared for the beauty of the Blue Ridge Mountains. During the first weeks of her stay, she sketched them with a new freedom. Then she added paint—large abstract images, mostly in black, gray, and white. The other artists at the colony were mainly realists, and mostly from the area. They hadn't seen anything like Elaine's work until then.

"What style is that?" asked Grant, a conservative realist who'd lived in the mountains his whole life. He was attracted to Elaine's work.

"Abstract expressionism," Elaine replied, cautiously. "Why?"

"I don't know. It's just unusual."

Elaine wasn't in a teaching mood. She avoided Grant and the others during most of her stay at the colony, especially as her condition became obvious. But when her water broke, it was Grant who drove her to the hospital.

"People are going to think you're the father, you know," Elaine said as Grant careened down the mountain road.

"I'm fine with that. You need someone, Elaine."

And so Grant witnessed what Willem would never see—a woman at her best and her worst, creating the highest form of art—bringing new life into the world.

"It's a girl!" The nurse handed the little red-faced being to Elaine, swaddled and shiny clean. Elaine nursed the baby against her better instincts. She knew it would be harder to leave her later, but she couldn't help herself (and couldn't really afford baby formula). She named the child Susannah Grace and called her Lily; Susannah meant "Lily of the Valley" in Hebrew.

• • •

Elaine swallowed her tears with another drink of Jack and pulled the next canvas from beneath the first one. She flattened it with her hands, anchoring the corners with paperweights. "Lily II" took her breath away, and she collapsed into her chair. She had forgotten about this one. An infant nursing at her mother's breast, her face looking up at her mother. One of her tiny hands kneading the breast while the other one reached toward her mother's face. The child's eyes were open wide, but the mother's eyes were closed. Again Elaine had used the palette knife and thick paint. Even the smallest details of the image had blurred edges, like the memory she had tried to erase.

When Lily was born, Elaine had looked into a nearby Catholic orphanage called Saint Agnes. The nun who met with her told her there were ten couples waiting to adopt every orphaned baby throughout the country.

Again she thought back ...

• • •

"I'm not sure I want to give her up for adoption." Elaine clung to Lily as she faced the nun at the orphanage.

"I understand, but raising a child as a single mother is difficult."

"What about the orphanage?" Elaine had hesitated, her own words sounding horrible to her ears. "Do you accept children for long-term care here?"

"Why would you do that? Your child could grow up in a loving home."

"I—I need some time. I'm not certain I can bring her into my world back home."

"Well, we don't take infants under three months for foster care. You've got a little time to decide."

There were calls from her artist friends in New York asking when she was returning, and invitations to show her new work began coming in. When her friend Grace Hartigan called, Elaine knew what she must do.

"When are you coming *back,* sweetie? We were talking about you last night at the Tavern. Everyone was there—Jackson, Franz, even Willem."

"Bill's back in New York?"

"Yeah—you haven't heard from him?"

Elaine's heart sank. She imagined Grace enjoying her place as one of a very few female artists accepted into the circle previously reserved for men.

"Sure—we've been in touch. But I didn't know he was already back from Maine."

"Just back. But listen, Jackson wants to show your work—and mine—in the New Talent Show at the Kootz in April. Get back here."

"How did this happen?"

"Dunno. Clement may have had something to do with it."

Clement. Elaine hadn't thought about him at Black Mountain. Their lovemaking had been mediocre the last time they were together. But he always said she was wonderful. More importantly, he thought her art was wonderful. And now—

"Thanks for the good news, Grace. I'll be home in a week or

so. I need to tie up some, uh, loose ends."

"How's the work going? Will you be bringing back lots of new pieces?"

"Um, I'm not sure. Mostly sketches. Ideas for new paintings."

"Sounds intriguing, darling. Well, give me a call when you get back."

"Thanks, Grace."

She hung up the phone and looked at Lily, asleep in the small bassinet she had bought at a flea market. *Loose ends. Is that what this sweet girl is? Am I a horrible person, or just a horrible mother?* But Lily was three months old. It was time. And the nun in the office was cool and efficient.

"Just a few more papers to sign. Remember, we can't keep your child for more than a year unless you relinquish your rights to her."

"I know. You've made that clear."

The nun paused, set down her pen, placed her elbows on the desk and touched her fingertips together, leaning on them slightly with her chin. She looked like she was about to pray.

"You can still release her for adoption, although her chances of being adopted will go down as she gets older," she said with more urgency. "A three-month-old is still considered an infant. We would have *no* trouble placing her."

"No. I—I can't. I can't just now ..." Elaine couldn't meet the nun's eyes. She picked up her child and held her tightly. "I'll be back, Lily." She kissed her, placed her in the bassinet, and hurried out the door. She held back her tears until she reached the car.

• • •

Unable to continue viewing the paintings, Elaine quickly rolled them up and put them away, locking the cabinet. She didn't remember finishing off the bottle of whiskey, but when she woke up the next morning—still in her office—she wished that was all she didn't remember.

Opening a file drawer, she pulled out a manila folder and placed it on top of her desk. Inside were copies of the papers she had signed in 1949, when Lily was one year old—papers to release her into the care of adoptive parents. But just as the nurse had warned her, most couples only wanted newborns, and Lily ended up spending her childhood at the orphanage. Elaine read the headlines from the yellowed newspaper clippings she had saved over the years:

NUNS AND PRIESTS ACCUSED OF
ABUSING ORPHANS

FIFTEEN-YEAR-OLD ORPHAN FLEES
FROM SAINT AGNES

ORPHANAGE CLOSES DOORS DUE TO
ALLEGATIONS OF ABUSE

Allegations. Nothing had ever been proved; the Catholic Church had simply moved the nuns and priests to another orphanage somewhere in Kentucky.

By this time Elaine's career had taken off in New York. No one knew anything about the child left behind in the mountains. She had tried to erase the memories with a successful career and a party life not unlike her own mother's. The year 1963—when she painted Kennedy's portrait just before he was killed—would carry the reminder that her own daughter had gone missing, possibly escaping horrors she never wanted to consider. Elaine had been fairly successful in blocking out those years until she met Mare.

Now she had to know what had happened to Lily—her daughter.

She had no idea where to begin. The orphanage had been closed for years. Would the *Asheville Citizen* have any information? Elaine called the paper and asked to speak to someone in archives.

"How far back?" a gruff-sounding man said.

"Excuse me?"

"How far back is the information you need?"

"Oh—well, let's see. 1963?"

"That was a long time ago. This could take some time."

"I really need your help," Elaine said, and explained, after an instant's hesitation, about her daughter and the orphanage and her desire to find out what happened to her. She was in tears by the end. The man on the other end was a lot less gruff when he replied.

"I'll be happy to go look. Can you hold?"

"Of course."

Elaine lit a cigarette and paced back and forth behind her desk, waiting with the phone in one hand and the cigarette in the other. Finally the voice returned.

"Did you say she was fifteen?"

"Yes, why? Do you have something?" Elaine felt a lump growing in her throat.

"Well, the only thing I see isn't really related to the orphanage. But the same year, a group of hippies started that religious commune down in Georgia—Heaven's Gate. The one where those people committed mass suicide, if you remember. In 1972."

Oh my God. Elaine felt like she might throw up. She put out her cigarette in the ashtray on her desk and sat on the edge of her chair with her head in her hands.

"Are you still there, ma'am?"

"Yes ... thank you."

"Anything else I can help with?"

"The mass suicides—um, were there survivors?"

"Let me cross check. We have other AP articles from that date. It might take a few minutes. Can you hold?"

Elaine tried to breathe. "Sure."

After what seemed an eternity, the man spoke again. "Okay. Are you still there?"

"Did you find anything?"

"Only this: the day of the suicides, a young girl was abandoned at the Department of Child Services in Monroe County."

"You're talking about Georgia, right?"

"Yes ma'am. A rural area near Macon."

"I can't thank you enough, sir. You've been very helpful."

Elaine's heart raced as she hung up the phone. She started to reach for another cigarette, realized the pack was empty, and swatted it to the floor.

Mare's childhood. God help me.

Elaine wanted to call her at the monastery, but this needed to be done in person. And it was a short drive from Savannah up the east coast to the mountains of North Carolina.

SEVENTEEN

TO **TAL** **AN** *ton to TAL an ton to TA to TA to TAL an ton.*

The sound of the talanton pealed through the morning air and into the guesthouse. Mare looked at the alarm clock—it was indeed five in the morning. She heard hushed voices and footsteps in the hall, the door to the guesthouse opening and closing as others were leaving for the church service. Peeking through the window blinds, she saw the nuns and visitors walking to the chapel in the shadows, their movements reflecting the moon in the darkness of the morning. It was still an hour before dawn.

Shit, am I the only one not going? The services are optional. I'm not a damned nun.

Mare pulled the covers over her head and tried to go back to sleep. Then she remembered Mother Christina's kindness to her the night before, the haunting voice of Sister Susannah reading the life of Saint Mary of Egypt, and the priest anointing her with oil from the myrrh-streaming icon. Her hands still smelled like roses, she realized, from the oil.

I'm wide awake. I might as well go.

• • •

The icon of Mary of Egypt shone in the middle of the nave as Mare entered the chapel and slipped into the back row. She would not light a candle or venerate the icon this morning, she decided.

Nuns took turns reading, chanting verses unfamiliar to Mare. She observed the movements of the other visitors as they stood, sat, knelt, and made the sign of the cross at various times throughout the service. A couple of hours passed. The middle-aged woman sitting next to Mare nudged her—Mare realized she had fallen asleep.

Finally it was time for breakfast, which took place in the refectory. After a blessing Mare sat at a table with several others—she noticed that the nuns sat separately from the visitors. Mother Christina stood and began to read about Great Lent. Mare thought about the icon workshop that would begin in just over an hour and looked for Sister Susannah. There she was, sitting silent and withdrawn, at one of the nuns' tables.

When breakfast was over, the nuns began to clear the tables while the visitors left to prepare for the icon workshop. On the way back to the guesthouse, Mare noticed several people walking arm-in-arm and chatting in a familiar way. The middle-aged woman who'd nudged Mare awake during the morning service walked alone and appeared to be waiting for Mare at the door.

"Hi. I'm Katherine," she said. "Is this your first workshop?"

"I'm Mare. Yes, first time. You?"

Katherine motioned for Mare to enter ahead of her. "I've been attending the past few years. Where are you from?"

"I'm a student at Savannah College of Art and Design. But I've never painted—um, *written* an icon."

"You've got the language down," Katherine said in a motherly way. "Your art training will help with the technical aspects. But iconography is spiritual work. Which is why they encourage us to go to the church services and to be quiet during meals."

Mare bristled a bit. Was everyone here into all this religious stuff? But then she took a deep breath and concentrated on why she was here—she wanted to learn to paint icons (or at least learn more about them). *I can do that and be my own self, right?*

She followed Katherine to a large room. Two long tables had been set up for the workshop with white paper covering them. Paint brushes, mason jars filled with water, a gessoed board, and a placard with each student's name had been set out at each workspace. About a dozen people found their places. The instructor sat at a smaller table at one end of the room. Mare slid in next to Katherine and breathed deeply. This felt familiar, like a studio. She could do this.

A nun named Sister Gabriella, according to her placard, mixed some powdery red clay with warm water and glue, pouring it into small cups for each of the workshop participants. It smelled earthy—almost musty—unlike the scents Mare was used to in the studio at school, where oils and binders and turpentine permeated the air. She remembered reading how the clay helped the gold leaf stick to the icon boards, and she couldn't wait to try it herself. Once everyone was seated, Sister Gabriela stood.

"Good morning, everyone," she said. "I see lots of familiar

faces and some new ones. Why don't we introduce ourselves?"

Mare was among five or six newcomers. Everyone else seemed to be Orthodox or Catholic. Most were not artists—just people seeking a religious experience through writing icons. When it was her turn to introduce herself, her voice cracked as she spoke.

"I'm Mare—Mary Katherine Henry—from Savannah, Georgia. Well, I'm not really from Savannah, but I go to school there. At SCAD, Savannah College of Art and Design. I'm not Orthodox. I'm here to learn how to write icons."

Sister Gabriella smiled at Mare. Other faces in the room were blank. Mare cleared her throat and continued.

"Well, that's not completely true. I mean, it's true, but it's not the whole story. I've visited a couple of churches in Georgia that had icons. Something intrigued me. Especially Mary of Egypt. Father Mark suggested I come to the workshop and, well, here I am."

"Thanks, Mare. I know God will bless your time here."

When everyone had introduced themselves, Sister Gabriella asked the new people to come up to her desk and get copies of the prototype of the Archangel Michael, which they would be writing during the workshop.

"What about you guys?" Mare asked Katherine and another woman at her table. "Aren't you painting the Archangel Michael?"

"No, we did him during our first workshop," Katherine explained. "After your first time, you can choose which icon to do, once you learn how to mix your own pigments. New students do the same icon, since the instructor mixes the pigments and shows you how to do each stage during the workshop."

"So, which saints are you doing this year?"

The woman across from Mare pulled out a sketch of the Mother of God holding the baby Jesus in her lap. The child was looking up at his mother's eyes, and their cheeks were touching. Her right hand directed the viewer's eyes toward the child.

"I'm doing the Mother of God, Tenderness," the woman said.

Katherine's sketch surprised Mare. It was obviously Saint Mary of Egypt—the long messy hair and the tattered cloak.

"Oh, you're doing ... that's Mary of Egypt, right?"

Katherine smiled but said nothing. Mare felt a pang of something—envy? She was so drawn to the sketch that she didn't notice when Sister Gabriella began to give her first set of instructions for the morning session.

"Mare? Are you with us?"

"Oh, yes. Sorry."

"I just asked that returning students begin transferring the sketches you did at home and brought with you to the boards. Newcomers, please gather around my desk."

Mare joined the other new students and watched Sister Gabriella demonstrate how to transfer a sketch of Archangel Michael to a board, using carbon paper for the initial transfer. Then she showed them how to etch the lines into the wood with a stylus.

"Take your time with the transfer and etching," Sister Gabriella said. "It isn't a quick process, but it's important to be as accurate as possible with these early steps. The lines you carve into the wood will be your guides for the painting process."

The others returned to their tables, but Mare stayed behind. "Um, I was wondering if you would let me do Saint Mary of Egypt," she said. "I already know how to mix pigments. Learned at school."

"Iconography is a spiritual art, and every step of the process has a spiritual meaning," Sister Gabriella began. "There's a reason we begin with an angel rather than a saint like Mary of Egypt. Angels do not have bodies; they are all spirit and mind. They teach us to circle around God in every action of our lives, just as the curls circle their faces—moving inward, toward the center. It's a good practice to begin our iconographic journey with an angel, like the Archangel Michael. Later you may progress to icons of saints, of Christ, and of the Mother of God."

Well, when I leave here I'll paint whatever I want. Mare nodded and took her copy of the sketch of the Archangel Michael and cast a longing look at Katherine's work-in-progress.

An hour later Mare had finished transferring the sketch of Archangel Michael and etching the lines onto her board. Her hand was cramping from holding the stylus so tightly. Katherine saw her rubbing her hand and laughed gently.

"Don't worry. That was the hardest part, physically. Painting the clay is really fun."

Mare watched as Katherine floated the liquid clay onto the area where the gold leaf would be applied later, using what Sister Gabriella called the "puddling and pushing" method. First she dropped a bit of the clay onto the board, and then pushed it gently to spread it a bit—just across the top of the puddle—and repeated with another brushful. When it was finished Mare thought it was beautiful, all shiny like glass.

"Wow. That's cool." Mare picked up a brush and began the process with the icon of Archangel Michael. The work seemed easy to her, and she finished about the same time as the others at her table, just as Sister Gabriella announced it was time for lunch. Walking to the refectory with Katherine, Mare noticed Sister Susannah emerge from a small building behind the guesthouse.

"What's that little house out back?" Mare asked.

"That's the icon studio where Sister Susannah works on commissions."

"Commissions?"

"Yes. It's one way the monastery makes money to support the nuns who live here."

"I'd love to see her work—do they allow tours?" Mare was hoping for a different answer than the one Mother Christina had given her.

"I'm afraid not. Sister Susannah works in seclusion."

"Why?"

"I'm not sure—Mother Christina told me it has something to do with her past," Katherine replied. "The nuns don't talk about their former lives once they come here."

• • •

After lunch Sister Gabriella gave lessons in applying gold leaf. Sanding, burnishing, and gilding took up the rest of the day. Just as she was finishing the halo, Mare heard again the sound of the talanton, calling everyone back to the church for evening prayers. Exhausted but mesmerized by the beauty of the afternoon sun reflecting off the halo she had just gilded, Mare followed the others into the chapel.

Prayers, meals, icon painting; prayers, meals, icon painting; the rhythm of the days drew Mare into the world of the icons— windows to Heaven. She resisted at first, still angry with a God who might not exist for all the pain she'd endured. But each day brought progress through the stages of painting an icon.

Once the first layer of paint—*roshkrish*, a Russian term for "chaos"—was floated onto the icon (using a technique similar to the puddling-and-pushing Mare learned in applying the clay), she painted lines to give order to the chaos. Now she understood why it was important to do a good job etching the lines in with the stylus. Otherwise she wouldn't be able to see the lines after covering them with the first layer of paint.

"Your work is very good, Mare," Sister Gabriella said over her shoulder as she went around the room supervising each student's work. "Your training at SCAD is helping you here."

"Thank you. I have a good teacher. Have you heard of Elaine

de Kooning? She came down from New York to teach for a few semesters at SCAD."

"Yes, I know that name."

"Anyway, this was the easiest part so far. I like painting the lines."

Sister Gabriella stood beside Mare for a minute longer. "I would mention that your lines are much darker and thicker than usual. I know you have the skill to make them thinner. See the prototype? Is this intentional?"

Mare felt the blood rush to her head. *Am I messing up already? Damn, there are so many rules.* "Well, the truth is, I really like the style of the Coptic icons better. I was following my gut. Couldn't help myself."

Sister Gabriella smiled. "I like the Coptic icons, too. It's just that we're teaching this workshop based on the Russian style. What you've done is kind of a hybrid—you've mixed two styles in one icon."

"Is ... is that wrong?"

"I once asked a priest how I would know if an icon is good or not, and he said it's good if you can pray before it. Style, method, and expertise—all that is secondary to the spiritual value of the icon." She stood quietly for a minute. Her eyes scanned the icon. Then she smiled. "Yes, I could pray before this icon."

"Then can I leave the lines as they are?" Mare knew she sounded almost childlike.

"Of course." Sister Gabriella patted Mare gently on the shoulder and moved on to help other students.

• • •

The first stages of icon painting were similar to the techniques Mare had learned at SCAD. But the highlights were a whole different process. As Sister Gabriella explained, the first high-light represented the light of nature (or the *cosmic* highlight), which indicated the natural light of the universe and revealed the basic sculptural shape of the figure. This first highlight also served as supportive under-painting for the smaller and livelier second and third highlights that followed. Floats, or light washes of intense color, were done next.

"This part is fun," Mare confided to Katherine, who was hard at work on her icon of Saint Mary of Egypt but paused to look at Mare's work.

"Yes, I love floating. The highlights seem to come alive through the floats, don't they?"

Next, the smaller and more specific highlights were applied within the first lights—representing something Sister Gabriella called the Anthropos, or the enlivening light of human intellect and culture.

"On the garments, the second highlight provides a sense of tension and action, as though the angel or saint has just moved," Sister Gabriella explained. "These facet-like second highlights on the garments are like looking into the depths of a crystal. They suggest the presence of other dimensions."

Mare painted the geometric-shaped highlights on the Archangel Michael's red garment. She was not sure she was experiencing "the presence of other dimensions," but the work began to come more naturally to her, and the icon seemed to come alive with each stroke of her brush.

"The third highlight symbolizes the Theocosm, the spiritual or angelic light," Sister Gabriella continued. "It is much smaller than previous highlights, reinforcing and embellishing them."

As Mare worked with ochre and white pigments to brighten the areas on the angel's cheeks, nose, and forehead, the angel's face began to take on an otherworldly glow. As she finished the highlights on the angel's wings—using a tiny brush and swift, expert strokes—she sat back and looked at it from a distance.

"Cool!"

Everyone giggled quietly at Mare's spontaneous outburst of excitement, and she felt her face turn as red as Archangel Michael's garment.

"Just wait until you see it after you repaint the lines and put in the life-giving lights," Katherine whispered to Mare. "You'll really think it's cool."

"Life-giving lights?" This sounded a bit too mystical for Mare, but maybe not when compared with the weeping icon that had been sitting on the stand inside the chapel all week.

"Ah, yes, the life-giving lights," Sister Gabriella said, approaching. "They're actually an extension of the third highlight, and we use them with the utmost discretion. May I demonstrate on your icon, Mare?"

Okay, mine because it's good, or because I need more help? Again Mare thought of Elaine, her mind jumping to the many times she'd called on her mentor for assistance. She brought her icon up to Sister Gabriella's table, and the new students gathered around and watched as the nun made a few subtle strokes—especially around the eyes, cheeks, and mouth of the angel.

"Now, Mare, you finish it."

Mare picked up the brush and continued the process, ending with the addition of the whites of the eyes. Her hand was shaking as she began to make tiny, moon-shaped strokes on the sides of the pupils with titanium white paint. She let out another loud breath as she finished, again soliciting quiet laughter throughout the room.

"That's all for today," Sister Gabriela said, perhaps taking Mare's reaction as a cue to wrap things up. "Take a short break before Vespers. Walk along the path by the cemetery and through the woods. Watch for the deer that often come out on the other side of the field at dusk—if you walk quietly and slowly, you might get close enough to see them eating the vegetables the sisters put out for them."

After cleaning her brushes and taking one last look at her icon, Mare headed outside. The others had started their walk. Mare was craving a smoke, so she walked down the gravel driveway toward the road and lit up, her mind spinning with all the new information she was processing. But even in the midst of everything she was learning about iconography, she couldn't quit thinking about Sister Susannah. When she finished her cigarette she walked back toward the guesthouse and down to the steps to the icon studio where the reclusive nun worked. She hid behind a tree about six feet from the back of the studio. It was beginning to get dark outside, and the lights inside the studio were bright. Peering into the windows, she saw Sister Susannah working on a large icon. It appeared to have several figures, a scene from the Bible, perhaps. Mare remembered Katherine's words:

Sister Susannah lives in solitude for a reason.

The nun's face was partly blocked by her habit, and she wore wire-rimmed glasses. But Mare again felt something familiar and compelling about this woman. As she crept closer to the studio, she tripped on a branch and felt against a tree. She tried to muffle her groans, but the noise caused Sister Susannah to look out the open window and directly at Mare. Their eyes locked for a moment. Then Mare hurried away, embarrassed for having intruded, and ran for the guesthouse when she heard the door of the studio open.

EIGHTEEN

AN HOUR LATER Sister Susannah was at the chanter's stand in the chapel again, chanting the appointed verses for the day. All the verses seemed to be about sin, and repenting. Well, Mare wondered, where was the judgment of God on those who had sinned against *her*? Where was God when her father was abusing her in His name back at Heaven's Gate? Where was God when Uncle Miles was raping her in his drunken rages? Mare was not sure what sin she needed to repent. Okay, defacing public property with her graffiti pieces wasn't a good thing to do, but hadn't she atoned for that by helping paint the mural at the church in Macon?

She tried to join the nuns and visitors as they said the Prayer of Saint Ephraim:

O Lord and Master of my life, take from me the spirit of sloth, despondency, lust for power and idle talk.

Everyone made a prostration—kneeled and got back up in a smooth movement.

But grant unto me, Thy servant, a spirit of chastity, humility, patience and love.

Another prostration.

Yea, O Lord and King, grant me to see my own faults and not to judge my brother. For Thou art blessed unto ages of ages. Amen.

A third prostration.

Not to judge my brother. Mare pondered this phrase. Did God expect her to forgive her father and Uncle Miles? And her mother? She had tried not to think about her mother these past few years, how she abandoned her. Maybe her mother hadn't been able to help it. If she was even alive today, where was she? She had promised to come back for Mare when she got clean and sober ... four long years ago.

Mare closed her eyes and listened with twelve-year-old ears for her mother's voice. Instead she heard this mysterious nun, Sister Susannah, chanting scripture. What had this woman done that led her to spend the rest of her life in seclusion, repenting and painting icons?

• • •

On Saturday, the final day of the icon workshop, Father Mark arrived. A big smile broke across Mare's face when he entered the studio.

"Father Mark! Thanks so much for recommending this workshop," she said.

"You made it! I'm so glad! How's your week been?"

"Real good. I've learned so much. And the nuns are helpful." *Except for Sister Susannah, who can't talk to anyone.*

"I'm glad. What about the church services?"

"Yeah ... you didn't tell me how long they last." Mare gave him a friendly smile. "And the weeping icon. So powerful I passed out—I kid you not."

"You had to experience it for yourself, Mare. Being at the monastery is about so much more than painting icons. But I imagine you're figuring that out. Oh, by the way, your professor—Mrs. de Kooning—called. She might come up for a visit this weekend."

Mare didn't try to hide her surprise. "Elaine? Visit the monastery?"

"Yes. I guess she wants to see how your work is going."

Mare thought Father Mark sounded odd—and looked uncomfortable—as he said this. But her mind quickly flashed back to Elaine's conversation about the time she spent at the artist colony almost forty years ago. "Hmm ... when's she getting here?"

"I think today. Anyway, don't want to interrupt you—may I see your icon?"

"Oh, sure." Mare was suddenly a bit shy about showing her work, but she led Father Mark to her table.

"Wow. Holy Archangel Michael." Father Mark made the sign of the cross. This caught Mare a bit off guard; it hadn't really occurred to her until now that what she was doing might be considered sacred—that her icon might be something holy.

"Cool, huh? This whole process is really amazing. We finish today."

"Yes. Sister Gabriella has asked me to bless them tomorrow after the church service."

"*Bless* them?"

"With holy water and special prayers."

Her artwork blessed? Mare wasn't sure how she felt about that. It was just a painting, right? *But that icon in the chapel that's been weeping is also just a painting.* Yet something miraculous was happening through it.

Students spent the morning painting the details on their icons—the names of the saints or angels whose images were represented, and decorative touches on various parts of the icons. Mare liked the abstract designs that some students painted in the borders. Others chose simple leaves and flowers to embellish their work. Since most steps of icon painting were guided by rules, it was fun to finally get to exercise a little creative freedom.

After lunch, Sister Gabriella taught the new students how to seal their icons with olifa, a special oil prepared by mixing linseed oil and stand oil. It came as no surprise that this step also had a spiritual meaning.

"The oil represents the oil of Chrismation," Sister Gabriella said. "When a person is united to the Church, they are anointed with Holy oil, or Chrism. In a way, this is the icon's Chrismation."

Following Katherine's example, Mare poured the oil over her icon in a movement imitating the sign of the cross, and then spread it with her hands. The colors, lines, and highlights began to jump out at her with even more brilliance than before, as the oil covered the surface of the icon and soaked into its luminous layers.

"How long does it take to dry?" Mare asked aloud.

"We'll spend the afternoon coaxing it along," Sister Gabriella replied. "Every fifteen minutes or so we'll take a little of the oil off the top with our hands, until it begins to feel a little tacky. Then we'll stop and let the icons dry."

Every fifteen minutes? Mare thought about how every aspect of writing icons in this ancient way was so organic and labor intensive. The process, according to Sister Gabriella, was supposed to help the iconographers connect themselves with the spiritual world. Mare wasn't so sure of that, but she felt her icon of Archangel Michael might be the most beautiful thing she'd ever seen. She couldn't tell anyone this, of course; such a declaration would go against the whole humility thing they had going here.

NINETEEN

ELAINE BATTLED WITH herself as she prepared to leave for the monastery. *I can do this. I must.* It wasn't the drive she dreaded. It was what she had to face at the end of the journey. And Father Mark hadn't been very helpful when she called him two days ago to ask for directions to the monastery.

"Why are you going?"

"I need to see Mare about something," she'd replied, pacing and smoking. "It's personal. It's complicated."

"You know the icon workshop is almost over, right?"

"Yes, it ends Saturday."

"Can't this wait until she returns to Savannah? The workshop is very intense. It's more than a painting class, Elaine. It's meant to be a spiritual retreat as well. I'm not sure you should interrupt. Can you tell me more about it?"

Taking a deep breath, Elaine recounted the events of the past—her past, and what turned out to be Mare's past as well.

"So, now you see why it's important for me to visit her at the monastery," she said quietly. "And I need to try to find Lily."

Father Mark was quiet on the other end of the phone for a long moment. "Yes, you probably do need to make this trip," he finally answered. "When are you leaving?"

"First thing Saturday morning."

"I'm driving up there tomorrow, so I'll meet you. God give you safe travels."

"Thank you very much, Father. I'll see you there."

• • •

Waking an hour before her alarm rang, Elaine dressed, tossed her bag into the car and headed out of Savannah before the sun came up. She knew she couldn't have slept more than a couple of hours amid all the tossing and turning overnight, but she'd gotten by on limited rest many times and would do so today. She stopped for gas and refilled her coffee thermos about halfway to Black Mountain, her mind racing back four decades to the artist retreat she used as cover for the birth of her daughter, Susannah Grace. Now her history converged with Mare's in the place where their lives unknowingly began to intersect all those years ago—Saint Agnes Home for Girls. The monastery was only another five or ten miles down the road, but she had to make this stop first.

She pulled off the road at the weathered sign. Winding down the gravel road, she came to the gate. Powerful memories came crashing down on her at the sight of the building.

She got out of her car, climbed over the gate, and walked down the driveway to the front of the abandoned building.

Approaching the front steps, she remembered the first time she had made that climb—pregnant with her daughter, alone and confused. Subsequent visits with the staff had culminated in her final trip, depositing Lily into the care of the nuns so that she might return to her life in New York City. She touched the railing and peered into the clouded windows, unable to see the rooms inside where her life—and her daughter's—were changed forever.

She knocked, though she didn't know what she was expecting—maybe a homeless squatter to greet her at the front door? When no one answered, she tried the knob, but it was locked. She banged on the windows as tears flooded her eyes.

"Lily! I'm so sorry!" she cried out. "Please forgive me! I am so, so sorry!"

Her words echoed back to her in the silence of the abandoned building—there wasn't even a birdsong to comfort her. Exhausted by the weight of the guilt she had carried for nearly four decades, she leaned against the front door and let her back slide down until she was crumpled in a heap on the dirty floorboards of the porch. Minutes later, as she found her way back to her car, she took one last look at the orphanage. What would she say to Mare when she saw the poor girl? Would Father Mark be able to help somehow, or did Elaine need to sit down with Mare one on one? More importantly, could Father Mark help Mare, depending on how she reacted?

• • •

When she arrived at the monastery, Elaine couldn't believe she hadn't known the place existed when she was at the artist colony. Several prominent buildings—including the chapel with its tall roof, dome, and cross—rose before her. The buildings were sitting on several beautiful acres. How could she have missed all this? Then again, it was hidden away on the back roads of the mountains and, well, she wasn't looking for God back then. Hell, she wasn't looking for Him today, either, she admitted to herself. Forgiveness, maybe, even redemption, but God wasn't the answer to what she was seeking. Getting out of her car, she saw a young nun walking across the grounds.

"Excuse me. Can you tell me where the office is, please?"

"Right over there." The nun pointed to a door at one end of a long, wooden building to the left of the chapel. "Are you looking for someone in particular?"

"Yes ... no ... I mean, I need to talk with Father Mark, the priest from Atlanta. Has he arrived?"

"I think I saw him talking with Mother Christina. Her room is right next to the office." Just as she pointed in that direction, Father Mark came walking out the door. "Oh—there he is now." Elaine watched as the nun walked toward Father Mark, bowed slightly, and asked his blessing.

"God be with you, Sister," Father Mark said, and made the sign of the cross and placed his right hand in her open palm. She kissed his hand and walked away silently. Then Father turned to Elaine. She knew he'd seen her, and she felt uncomfortable in the face of what she considered an almost pious show of respect from the nun, but Father Mark was certainly used to dealing with non-Orthodox visitors to his parish in Atlanta. He looked honestly glad to see her and came walking up with a friendly smile.

"Great to see you again, Elaine. Did you have any trouble finding the place?"

"No, not really. Thanks to your good instructions." Elaine looked around the grounds. Several nuns and visitors were walking nearby. "Um, is there some place we can talk?"

"Sure. Let's go to the common room in the guesthouse. It's right over here."

Elaine followed Father Mark inside. As they entered the building, he pointed down a hallway to the left. "That's where the icon workshop is being held."

Elaine was anxious to see Mare and her work, but the talk with Father Mark was urgent. She followed him into the common room, where several couches and chairs and small tables were scattered about. A kitchenette in one corner was furnished with a small refrigerator. A coffee pot was next to the sink with several cups alongside, face down on a dish towel. Father Mark led Elaine to a table near a window.

"Would you like some coffee?"

"No, thanks. I finished several thermoses on the road today."

Father Mark still looked friendly and encouraging. But he was quiet now, waiting for her to speak her mind. She stared at her hands and finally at his face.

"Oh, Father, I am so ashamed. I can't believe I've lived with myself all these years. How can you bear to look at me?"

"Elaine, I'm a priest. I hear confessions. Nothing shocks me."

"Is that what this is—a confession?"

"Well, not formally. But God hears the utterances of our hearts no matter where we are. Is there more you want to tell me than what you related on the phone?"

"No, not really. I have to know if my daughter is here. If she's willing to meet with me. Did you speak with the abbess?"

"That's where I was when you arrived—"

"And?"

"—Mother Christina is talking with one of the nuns right now." He paused. "Who might be your daughter."

The room started to spin. Elaine stood up ... and nearly fell as dizziness set in. Father Mark was suddenly on his feet and had her arm.

"I can ... barely breathe ..."

"Here, sit back down. I'll get you some water. This is difficult, but I thank God you're dealing with it, Elaine—and here's Mother Christina now."

The door opened. The nun who joined them was small—just over five feet tall and very slender—but carried herself with a sense of authority. Just as Elaine was beginning to feel intimidated, the woman's face lit up with a compassionate smile. Elaine remained seated, blinked several times, and gladly accepted a coffee cup that Father Mark had rinsed and filled with tap water. As she drank, Mother Christina pulled a chair next to her, sat beside her, and put her arm around her shoulder.

"You must be Elaine."

• • •

Elaine didn't answer. She couldn't move. She couldn't think. She couldn't speak. *Where did all the air go?* She closed her eyes and tried to clear her head. It had been hard enough telling Father Mark what she'd done, and now she had to face a nun with her failings. Finally, she took a breath, eased over a foot or so closer to Mother Christina, and looked her in the eye.

"Is she here, really? My daughter—is she—is she one of your nuns?"

"We believe so, Elaine. I've just spoken with her."

Oh my God. "Does she know I'm here? Is she willing to meet me?"

"Of course. Why wouldn't she be?"

Elaine began to cry. "I—I'm so ashamed. All those years ago. How could—how could she forgive me?"

Mother Christina turned Elaine toward her. "We all have painful things in our past, Elaine. Some of us bring them to the monastery. That's what Sister Susannah did."

"Sister *Susannah*? That's her name? Oh, my gosh, I named her Susannah Grace, but I called her Lily, hoping she would always be joyful or bright. But oh, how could she be?" Elaine slumped down in her chair, coughing and short of breath. She felt her whole self was caving in. "Leaving her there in that orphanage ... the horrible things that happened there ..."

Mother Christina hugged Elaine. Father Mark, still on his feet, handed her a box of tissues.

"Thank you, Father." Elaine took one tissue, then another, as she blew her nose and continued to weep. After she drew a few ragged breaths and calmed down, she listened to Mother Christina.

"Sister Susannah understands the need for forgiveness. She also abandoned a daughter. And she carries an even heavier weight—she wasn't able to save her two sons. She did the best she could under the circumstances."

"The—the *circumstances*? That cult in Georgia where the mass suicide took place?" Elaine's brain felt like it was on speed. "How did she get there? Did she run away from the orphanage, or what?"

Mother Christina patted Elaine on the shoulder. "Let's take it slow. There's a lot to understand. It took Sister Susannah a long time to share her story with me. But she wants you to know what happened."

"She wants *me* to know?" Elaine looked at Father Mark. "So she knows I'm here?"

"I told Mother Christina your part of the story, Elaine," the priest replied. "Sister Susannah needed to know. She wants to work through this with you, together."

"She wants to see you, Elaine," Mother Christina said. "She's in the icon studio out back waiting for you. Would you like to go there now?"

Elaine nodded and tried to wipe her tears away.

"Father Mark will take you, then. I have Vespers now. I'll join you later."

"What about Mare?" Elaine asked.

"Later," Mother Christina answered, and smiled. "One step at a time."

• • •

By late afternoon Mare's icon was dry enough to leave alone overnight. She covered it with an inverted box to keep dust from settling into the surface as the oil finished sealing the pigments. Exhausted but happy, she headed to her room to rest before evening services. Father Mark was here, so she knew she should make an appearance. She heard a familiar voice as she passed by the common room near the front of the guesthouse and stuck her head inside. Sure enough, there was Elaine in conversation with Father Mark. Seeing her was a surprise, even though the priest had mentioned it.

"Hi, Elaine!"

"Uh, hi, Mare ..."

Mare thought Elaine's smile looked a little awkward, like she had something to hide. "What are you doing here? I mean, Father Mark said today that you were coming, but you didn't mention it to me, so ..."

"I couldn't wait to see your work."

"Well, the icons are down the hall. Want me to show you?"

"Uh, Father Mark and I have some things to discuss. How about after dinner tonight?"

Things to discuss? "Sure. Whatever," Mare said. She could tell she was not to be included in the conversation, so she headed to her room. Feeling confused and left out, she plopped down on the bed and tried to figure out what was going on.

Soon she heard footsteps outside the window. Opening the curtain, she saw Father Mark and Elaine walking down the steps and off toward the icon studio where Sister Susannah worked. Mare wasn't sure whether it was curiosity or jealousy, but something uncomfortable was building inside her.

What the hell?!?

She recognized the emotion as anger, or at least a degree

of it. Elaine, after all, had made a big point (more than once) of saying she'd never been religious, yet here she was having a private conversation with Father Mark—at a monastery—and then going with him to Sister Susannah's private icon studio.

Where no one was allowed.

Mare looked at the clock. It was half an hour until Vespers, and there sure wouldn't be a nap with this clandestine activity going on. She pulled on a jacket, tiptoed out the door, and started down the path. Father Mark and Elaine were inside the studio when she arrived. Hidden from view by the ensuing darkness, she peered through an open window and saw the three of them talking. She felt her eyes widen as Sister Susannah and Elaine embraced—what the hell was this about? Father Mark, Mare saw, walked out of the room, and she stepped away from the window and prepared to confront him when he stepped outside.

"You want to tell me what's going on, Father?"

"Mare." She'd clearly startled him. "What are you doing out here?"

"Answer my question. Why is Elaine in there with Sister Susannah, hugging like long-lost friends? What's going on?"

Father Mark offered Mare a hand. "Let's head up to Vespers and leave them to their business. You'll get to visit with them both later."

"No!" Mare pulled her hand away from Father Mark and crossed her arms. "I'm not going anywhere until someone tells me exactly what's happening."

Father Mark took a deep breath and stared at Mare, who wasn't budging from her defiant stance. "You're just going to have to trust me, Mare. No one is trying to shut you out, but this is the way it needs to happen. Elaine and Sister Susannah need some time to talk first. You'll get to talk with them after Vespers. I promise."

Something in Father Mark's voice reached down into a place

that Mare hadn't accessed in a long time, maybe ever.

She found herself believing him.

But she drew the line at going to another church service until this was settled. "Fine," she muttered. "I'll be in my room. If anyone cares."

Mare, however, headed out to the pasture beyond the chapel and toward the woods. The full moon began to light up the field. Mare looked around. No one was in sight, and she lit a cigarette and stood looking at the beauty of her surroundings. She saw three deer, silhouetted on the path in front of her. They saw her, too, before they scampered back into the woods. Mare watched their white tails disappear and wondered if their quick departure was a sign.

"Maybe that's what I should do, too," she whispered into the silence, exhaling smoke into the sky. "Hurry home to safety. Problem is, I have no home. Elaine's the closest thing I've known to family in a long time. And Father Mark has been kind. Maybe I should trust them.

"Maybe."

TWENTY

FATHER MARK AND Elaine walked toward the guesthouse and down the steps to Sister Susannah's private studio. Its light cast a warm glow on the darkening woods and the path near the door. Through the window Elaine saw Sister Susannah sitting at her drawing table. She wasn't painting. She wasn't sketching. She was just sitting quietly, her head bowed. *My daughter.* Her lips were moving as she fingered the knots of a prayer rope in her lap.

Father Mark knocked on the door. Sister Susannah rose as they entered and promptly asked him for a blessing. Hearing her soft, sweet voice for the first time brought a rush of emotions to Elaine. Susannah sounded like a young girl—or was that just because Elaine knew she was listening through the filter of a lifetime of not hearing that voice?

Sister Susannah looked at Elaine. For an instant neither of them spoke, or moved. Then she—*Lily*—rushed to hug her. It was the last thing she'd expected, but here her grown daughter was, weeping loudly with her head against Elaine's shoulder. She put her arms around Sister Susannah, gently at first, then pulled her into a firm hug.

"You came for me," Sister Susannah rasped. "I didn't think— it's been over forty years."

Elaine found her voice. "I know. How can you ever forgive me? I was so selfish ... I wanted my life to be a certain way. The worst thing a mother can do."

"No," Sister Susannah pulled back and faced her. "The worst thing is to let your children *die*. That's what I did. My sons ... I let their father kill them. I was too weak to stop him."

Now Elaine understood: Susannah *did* end up at Heaven's Gate.

She's Mare's mother!

Elaine clasped her hands to her chest to slow her breathing. As the events of their lives became clearer, she spoke her thoughts aloud without considering the impact of so much information all at once.

"But what about Mare? You saved her, didn't you?"

Sister Susannah looked surprised to hear her daughter's name, if not stunned.

"How—how do you know about Mare?

"She's a student at SCAD—Savannah College of Art and Design—where I'm a visiting professor. We've become close ... and now she's here at the monastery for the icon workshop. I thought you knew."

Sister Susannah looked at Father Mark, who nodded his agreement. Then she looked back at Elaine.

"A college student ... learning iconography ... *here*?"

Father Mark cleared his throat. "I need to get to Vespers. The two of you need some time alone. There's a lot of catching up to do."

"But what about Mare?" Elaine asked. "Don't we need to include her in this conversation?"

"After Vespers."

As Father Mark turned to leave, Sister Susannah caught him by the arm and said, "Pray for us, Father."

"Of course. I always do."

Silence filled the studio, broken only by the cooing of a dove just outside the window. The sun cast long shadows as it descended behind the woods.

"Would you like some tea?" Sister Susannah motioned toward a table in the corner of her studio, where an electric teapot, cups, and condiments were neatly laid out. Her movements, Elaine noticed, were almost mechanical. She took one of the chairs and watched Susannah heat the water and place the tea bags in their cups. It felt like a dream, like watching someone from beneath the surface of water.

"If it's no trouble," Elaine said. Suddenly she blurted out, "So, what do you remember—or what did the nuns tell you about me? At the orphanage, I mean."

"I don't remember you, if that's what you're asking. I was only three months old when you left."

"I know. But I was wondering what your life was like there, in the orphanage. I read about some terrible things that went on. I was so afraid you might have suffered." Elaine reached for her tea. Her hands were shaking so badly the cup rattled against the saucer when she tried to pick it up. She set it back down and placed her hands in her lap. She started to cry as she continued. "I wish—I wish I had kept you. Or signed those papers earlier. You might have been adopted into some nice home."

"We can't change the past." Sister Susannah handed Elaine

a box of tissues and sat down in the second chair by the table. "When I was old enough to ask, the nuns told me that you said you were coming back for me." She looked out the window, took a sip of her tea, and then looked at Elaine. "By the time I was four or five, I quit asking about you—"

Elaine's heart sank. *God help me.*

"—but it started when I was about five. One of the nuns would come and get me from my bed and take me to Father George's office. She told me I was special, that I had been chosen by Father George, that I was his favorite. After a while I learned that they said that to all the girls."

Elaine looked away from her daughter, unable to bear the pain she saw in Susannah's eyes as she described her abuse at the hands of the priests and nuns. It reminded her of her own difficult childhood. Had she visited her own suffering on two generations?

"He would make me sit in his lap and listen to him read the Bible. As I got older, he would make me recite Psalms or the Lord's Prayer. I could feel him getting hard under me. Then he began to put his fingers between my legs. I would beg him to stop, but he always just said, 'Keep praying, child,' and that's what I did. Until the rapes began."

Now it was Sister Susannah who needed the tissues, and she reached for the box on the table between them and dabbed at the tears that were starting to well up. Elaine wondered how she had handled her emotions—and anger—all these years. Did being a nun help? It seemed that Susannah, though relating a true nightmare of a childhood to her mother, wasn't letting herself completely fall apart. Elaine looked up from her lap.

"Didn't the nuns try to help you?"

"No. They were afraid of Father George. And some of them were mean. They beat us and humiliated us and kept food from us."

"Oh, Susannah, how did you get away? And when?"

"I was about fourteen. I got my period and Father George wouldn't touch me any more. He said I was dirty. The nuns made me clean the bathrooms and stay away from the younger girls. He—Father George—only wanted the younger ones. So, one night when everyone was asleep, I sneaked out of the orphanage and ran all the way to the highway.

"Just about dawn I saw a truck coming and hitchhiked a ride. Fortunately, the driver was kind. He let me ride with him all the way to Georgia. We stopped for gasoline and he bought me breakfast. On some county road in the middle of nowhere, I saw a sign across from the gas station that said, 'Heaven's Gate.' A young woman with children came out of the convenience store attached to the gas station and looked at me. The woman smiled, and then they disappeared across the highway and down the dirt road by the sign."

Heaven's Gate. It was the place Mare had told Elaine about. As Sister Susannah continued her story, it all began to make sense to Elaine.

"But when I came out of the restroom after breakfast, I noticed the truck driver talking to a policeman out behind the truck stop. I was afraid he was going to turn me in and I'd have to go back. So when he wasn't looking, I ran down the dirt road where the woman and children had gone. In a few minutes I came to the farm, and that's where I met Scott."

"Scott?"

"Yes. He was the leader at Heaven's Gate. There were dozens of hippies there, living in lean-tos and rotting cabins and trailers. Growing their own food, for the most part. Holding prayer meetings in an old barn they used for a chapel. They welcomed me. I thought I had found a safe place."

"But, it wasn't safe, was it?" Elaine pushed her cup of tea aside and reached across the table and took Sister Susannah's hands. She didn't push them away, thankfully.

"No, Scott already had several 'wives.' He was charming and handsome and convinced me it was God's will, that God had brought me there to him. So I married him, if you can call it that. And we had three children—Phoenix, Jagger and Mare. You know Mare from teaching, right? How much has she told you about life on the farm?"

Elaine's mind rushed back to what Mare told her about growing up at Heaven's Gate, about her father's abuse, and about her eventual escape. The memories of Elaine's own childhood returned with a vengeance. Would the cycle ever end?

"She told me the whole story, Susannah. How brave you were to escape with her and save her—and yourself—from the mass suicides engineered by your husband."

Sister Susannah hung her head. "You make it sound like I was some kind of hero. I was just a drug addict who got lucky in a moment of sobriety."

"Lucky?" Elaine's grip on her daughter's hands tightened. "It took more than luck to do what you did. It took courage. Mare is alive because of you."

"I can't believe she'd speak to me. She has every right to be angry the rest of her life. I promised I would come back for her when I got clean, and I never did."

Elaine nodded. "Why was that? Why didn't you go back for her?" she asked gently. "Especially after the pain you lived with because I abandoned you?"

"I ... I don't know."

"And that's the best you can come up with? Come on, Susannah, I've owned my part in all this. I admitted it was my selfishness that led me to abandon you, hoping for the glamorous life of a successful artist in New York. As horrible as that is, it's the truth. I've come clean with you about it. I don't know if you can ever forgive me, but at least you know. Don't you think Mare deserves the truth from you?"

Sister Susannah let go of Elaine's hands and walked to the window. Darkness had fallen, and Elaine could see her daughter's reflection in the window. Any calm detachment Susannah had possessed moments ago was gone—Elaine clearly saw the pain her daughter was feeling. She joined Susannah at the window and put an arm around her shoulder.

"I'm here for you now," she whispered. "You can do this, Susannah Grace."

TWENTY-ONE

VESPERS WAS OVER. When Mare returned from her walk in the woods, images of the deer scampering away were still in her mind. She saw Father Mark and Mother Christina coming out of the chapel and knew it was time to stop running.

"Mare," Father Mark called out, waving at her from across the lawn.

Mare peered at them with a mixture of anticipation and fear. *Look, I still want to know what's with—*

"Mother Christina and I were thinking this would be a good time for you to talk with Elaine and Sister Susannah."

"You say their names like they're thick as thieves. I feel like the child who's been put to bed at the grownups' party."

The head nun and the priest exchanged a look, then approached her. Father Mark offered a hand, but Mare pulled back.

"Just tell me what's going on, okay?"

Mother Christina's voice was calm. "We want you to hear their side of the story. Let's head down to the icon studio."

Mare followed them down the path. She wiped her face on her shirtsleeve, like a tough kid who had just been in a fight. And wasn't that what her entire life had been?

"We think you should go in alone," Father Mark said at the end of the path. "We'll join you in a few minutes."

Mare couldn't speak. She stared as the two of them turned and walked away. Then she took a deep breath and opened the door of the studio.

• • •

She closed the door behind her quietly, blinked her eyes a couple of times, and took in the small room. Her eyes came to rest on the mysterious Sister Susannah and Elaine, who were chatting and smiling. Though it looked like Elaine had been crying—maybe both of them had. Elaine offered Mare her chair at the table by Sister Susannah.

"It's okay. I'd rather stand." Mare crossed her arms and backed against the wall several feet from the door. This was the first time she had seen Sister Susannah up close in a well-lighted room. "Now ... who are you?"

"I'm ... I'm your mother, Mare," Sister Susannah managed.

"No, you're *not*! I think I would know my own mother, even after four years."

Sister Susannah stood up and removed her glasses. Then she began to remove the pins holding her head covering in place. She pulled it off and placed it on the table. Finally she unpinned her long hair and shook it loose so that it landed softly on her shoulders. Mare watched this transformation with a mixture of wonder and disbelief. Then she turned to Elaine.

"And *you*! How did you know she was here? I mean, what business is this of yours?"

"Please, just sit down, Mare," Elaine said calmly. "We'll tell you everything."

Mare shook her head and held her stance by the wall.

"I know this is difficult for you, Mare. It's hard for all of us," Sister Susannah said, folding her hands on the table. Mare stared at the floor as her mother began to speak. "After I left you at Children's Services, I went to a rehab center for a few months to get clean. I got a job as a waitress for a while but still felt worthless, which is what your father always told me I was. I went through therapy, even took some prescription medicine. That's when I had the idea to go to a monastery. The nuns have been nursing me back to health. They encouraged me to learn iconography and taught me to chant in the church services. But most importantly, they helped me learn to forgive."

"Forgive *who*?" Mare almost shouted the question. She dropped her arms to her side and clenched her fists.

"Your father, of course, but also myself. For letting your ... your brothers die ... and for abandoning you."

"So why didn't you come back for me once you had all this forgiveness and religion going on?"

Sister Susannah held Mare's eyes before responding. "I don't expect you to understand right away, but it has taken me all this time to get to a place where I felt I could be a healthy influence in your life."

Mare, as she listened, felt as if she was watching her life story on microfilm, like when she was reading about graffiti at the library that summer back in Monroe County. Elaine took a deep breath, wiped her eyes, and looked at Mare with a new tenderness.

"I didn't just come here to see you, Mare. I came to find my daughter—Susannah. Meaning, Mare, I'm your *grandmother*."

"*What?*" She looked back and forth between the two women. "Am I just supposed to accept this and be happy about it? Two generations of bad mothers serving up tea and smiles—at a monastery of all places—as though the past doesn't matter? As though it never happened?"

Elaine stood and moved toward her. "Mare, listen—"

"No, *you* listen! My entire life has been fucked up because of the choices you two made."

Sister Susannah was crying openly now and pleading for forgiveness, possibly; she wasn't speaking aloud, but her lips were moving. Mare held her stance against the wall, though. She was going to get answers no matter whose feelings were hurt. The door opened then, and Father Mark and Mother Christina stepped inside. Sister Susannah hurried to pin her hair back up and replace her head covering and glasses. Mare turned to the priest.

"*You*! Did you know all of this when you suggested I come here? The icon workshop—was it a set-up or what?"

"No, Mare. It's a good place to learn iconography," Father Mark said calmly. "I promise I didn't know anything about the connections between the three of you."

Mother Christina's countenance set the stage for peace-making. "Mare, I think you should know that when Sister Susannah came here, she was in no shape to take care of herself, much less anyone else. Therapy and medication brought her to a place where she could receive spiritual healing. The reason she is still 'Sister' and not 'Mother' is because she did not want to take her full vows, in case she ever became strong enough to leave the monastery and look for you."

"That's fantastic," Mare said, looking at Sister Susannah and then back at Mother Christina. "All I know is, she never bothered to—"

"You see, when a nun takes her final vows, she agrees never to leave the monastery. Her relatives can visit her, but she can never go back to the outside world. Ever again. Sister Susannah recently asked permission to begin searching for you ... just before you showed up for the icon workshop, actually."

"How convenient."

"It's true, Mare," Mother Christina replied. Her face was so full of love that Mare, down deep, found it hard to believe the woman would ever lie. Sister Susannah stepped forward.

"Mare, honey, I—"

"*Don't* call me that." Mare turned and reached for the doorknob, but the floor beneath her feet began to feel like it was shifting. She closed her eyes and held onto the knob, trying to steady herself.

"Mare, please wait!" Now Sister Susannah was at her side. "You have every right to be hurt. To be angry with me. I've felt anger, too. I won't blame you if you leave. But I understand—"

"You can't *begin* to understand—"

"Oh, but I do. You're mad at God. You don't want to paint icons. You want nothing to do with the Church. But please ... don't give up on yourself. Return to SCAD. Continue your studies there. You have the potential to do something important."

Mare kicked at the floor. Then she looked at Elaine. "Will you even be at SCAD next year?"

"Yes. My contract is for two years—the rest of this semester and next year. I hope you'll give our relationship another chance."

"Can we just leave? Tonight? Right now?"

Elaine looked at Mother Christina, but it was Father Mark who answered.

"I hope you'll wait until tomorrow afternoon, Mare."

"Why?"

"I'll be serving Liturgy and preaching the sermon for the Feast Day of Saint Mary of Egypt tomorrow. I think it could be meaningful for you."

"Please stay, Mare," Mother Christina added.

Mare shrugged and said, "I'm finished with the workshop. That's why I came here."

"Fair enough," Father Mark replied. "But just so you know, Mare, tomorrow morning I will bless all the icons that have been written during the workshop—the ones that the students bring to church to have blessed, that is."

Mare sighed. *Is there no end to the religious crap?*

Elaine said, "Speaking of which—I haven't seen your icon yet, Mare. Can you show it to me tonight?"

"Okay, but do we really have to stay for tomorrow? Can't we spend the night partway to Savannah or something?"

"It's already late. We're both exhausted, emotionally and physically. Might not be safe for us to get on the road tonight. But if you want to leave first thing in the morning, that's fine with me."

Mare looked at Mother Christina. "I guess there's not a bus out of here tonight."

Mother Christina shook her head. "Only one a day, in the afternoon."

"Looks like I'm stuck till tomorrow, then. Come on, *Elaine.* I'll show you my piece."

• • •

As she and Mare entered the workshop where all the newly-oiled icons were drying, Elaine took in the familiar smell of pigments and gesso and the comforting sights of paint brushes and other tools of the trade, which she herself had spent a lifetime learning and teaching. They were alone in the workshop room where all the students' icons were left to dry from the oil with which they had been sealed earlier. Elaine walked over to Mare's table and spotted Katherine's icon first.

"Oh, I love this one!"

"Yeah, that's Katherine's. She's been a good friend to me during the workshop. I really like her stuff. Not my style, though."

Elaine nodded. "I can see that. Much more stylized than the Coptic icons you've been admiring. But it's beautiful, isn't it?"

Mare managed a smile. "I wanted to paint that icon—of Mary of Egypt—but Sister Gabriella said I should start with the Archangel Michael. It's the one she recommends for all new students."

Elaine couldn't help teasing her a bit. "And you were okay with that, I'm sure."

"Not at first, but when she explained the reasons, it kind of made sense. I decided not to put up a fuss." Mare removed the cover from her work. "Here's my icon."

Elaine stepped close to the table and leaned in to look at the details. "Oh, my. It's hard to believe this is your first one, Mare."

"Thanks. That's what some of the other students said. I guess I feel pretty good about it."

"I can see your primitive leanings at work here, even in a spiritual painting. Was the instructor okay with it?"

"I told her I loved the Coptic style, and she said to go for it. Well, not in those words."

Elaine stepped back to view the icon from a different angle. "This is good work, Mare. The lines are crisp and clear. The highlights are subtle, but effective. The eyes are nicely shaped. I love the details in the robe—in the sword, too." She paused. "You may think I'm saying this because of what just happened back there, but as your instructor, it's just wonderful, really."

"Thank you," Mare whispered. "That makes me feel good."

Elaine waited to see if Mare wanted to show her anyone else's work, but it didn't look like it, and Mare followed when she started for the workshop door. She hesitated, then went ahead with the question she would have asked had the few minutes with Susannah not been so explosive.

"Would it be okay, Mare, if we didn't leave until after church tomorrow?"

"Why do you care? I had to drag you to those churches in Macon and Atlanta so I could see the icons, remember?"

"I know, but this is different. I just found Lily—Sister Susannah—after all these years. I'd like some more time with her ... and you know she painted the icon that's weeping."

"The one in the chapel?"

"Yes. I haven't seen it yet, and I'd like to be there tomorrow. Just to show support for my daughter. I owe her that, and so much more, really."

Mare had paused. Now she turned. Elaine couldn't tell from the mirthless smile whether her granddaughter was angry or not. "Okay ... how do you know that my mother—excuse me, *Sister Susannah*—painted that icon? *Elaine?*"

"She told me. Tonight, in her studio."

"And was anybody going to tell *me* this?"

"She would have, Mare. If you'd given her the chance."

"Oh, for God's sake. So, what's the story? When—how did she paint it? Did she say anything about why it's weeping?"

Sister Susannah was suddenly in the doorway. "I'll tell you, Mare."

TWENTY-TWO

MARE HADN'T HEARD Sister Susannah—her *mother*—coming, and neither had Elaine, based on her look of surprise.

"What are you doing here?" Mare asked.

"I wanted to see the icon you painted," Sister Susannah replied. "I figured you might not bring it to church to have it blessed in the morning, and I really wanted to see it."

Mare felt a small part of her anger melt away. "It's over here. But you should see Katherine's. It's amazing." Mare moved back toward the table and removed the cover. Sister Susannah approached and gazed at the icon.

"Ah, yes, Holy Mother Mary of Egypt. Katherine does good work."

"You know her?"

"Oh, not personally. Sometimes Sister Gabriella asks me to give the students pointers during the workshops. Katherine has attended several."

"Why don't you teach the workshops?"

"I've needed to be alone. Mare. I was so—" Sister Susannah looked at Elaine before finishing her thought. "—wounded by what happened in my childhood. And then at the farm, with your father. I wasn't in any shape to teach others anything."

"And yet you painted an icon that weeps?"

Sister Susannah bowed her head. "Mother Christina thought writing icons would be healing for me. She asked Sister Gabriella to teach me."

"Wait—back up," Mare snapped. "The last time I saw you, you were strung out on drugs. You didn't stop Father from raping me at the farm. And then you dumped me at a welfare office."

"Oh, Mare—"

"Hey, you're *going* to hear this. I spent the rest of my so-called childhood with my foster father, 'Uncle Miles,' drunk all the time, *fucking* me when he wasn't beating me. Then I lived on the streets in Macon, hiding from the cops and throwing up graffiti. You were here, safe and clean, all that time. Painting icons. Singing in the monastery choir. While I was going through hell!"

Elaine walked over to Sister Susannah and put her arm around her. "Come here and sit down. Both of you."

For an instant Mare thought about marching out the door, going straight for her room, and refusing to budge until Elaine said they were leaving for Savannah. But she took a deep breath (*really* wishing she could have a cigarette), uncrossed her arms, and sat at the table with Sister Susannah and Elaine. The icons of Saint Mary and Archangel Michael stared up at them; the patron saint of penitents and the angel of protection were witnessing three generations as they worked to sort out the injustices in their lives. The matriarch's confession came first.

"Susannah didn't have an easy time, Mare," Elaine began. "Drug rehab was no cakewalk. She couldn't trust anyone for a long time. What she never told you—you were just a child—was that she was abused at that orphanage where I left her for all those years. That's the guilt I have to live with."

Mare closed her eyes for an instant. Then she focused on Sister Susannah—really *looked* at her for the first time—and saw the abandoned and abused child she once was, instead of the mother who deserted her. And then Mare asked what she had been wanting to know for a long time.

"Did ... did Father give you drugs at the farm?"

"Yes."

"And did he rape you, the way he raped me?"

"He did. Oh, Mare, I was so messed up and confused about what my role was. I don't even know if we were legally married. Your father made all the rules. We were all brainwashed. We just obeyed him. I should have protected you. I was the adult, you were a child. Now, I believe that God has forgiven me, but I don't know how you will ever be able to."

"I'm trying. I really am," Mare said to both of them. "It's going to take time. You still haven't explained everything—like how you painted an icon that weeps."

"After I had been here a few months, Mother Christina asked Sister Gabriella to teach me to paint icons. As therapy. The work just came natural—I hadn't had any training. We were all surprised." She looked at Elaine. "It kind of makes sense now that I know my mother is an artist. When I did the icon of Saint Mary of Egypt, it started weeping ... right after I finished it. I was so afraid I almost ran away from the monastery."

Mare tried to picture this in her mind. "What—what did you do with it? With the icon?"

"Mother Christina took it to the cathedral so the bishop could see it. Several priests declared it miraculous—the icon *really* was weeping. So it stays at the cathedral, except on its feast day every year when they bring it here to the monastery."

"But what I don't understand is *why*. Why is it weeping?"

"Mother Christina says icons weep when the saint is sad about something. Most weeping icons are of the Mother of God. She weeps for all sorts of things—wars, the pain and suffering of mankind, all that. But this is the first weeping icon of Saint Mary *of Egypt* that we've heard of. Mother Christina thinks she might be weeping for me. And for other women and children who have been abused." Susannah paused. "Maybe she's weeping for you, Mare ... and for ... Elaine."

Mare looked at them both. How crazy—the three of them, who shared not only DNA but also histories of abuse—here at this monastery together, to witness a miraculous icon. All at once Mare felt absolutely flattened. She wasn't sure she could stand and walk back to her room, let alone ask any more questions.

"It's fine if we stay until after church tomorrow," she said to Elaine. "I'm going to bed."

• • •

Mare awoke to the sounds of the talanton, which had grown familiar to her as the week progressed. She felt, though, as if she had only been asleep a few minutes. After all, how could she sleep with everything that had happened? She rolled over and pulled her pillow over her head, trying to shut out the early morning sounds and the late night memories, but she wasn't able to do either successfully. Finally she rolled out of bed, remembering that she would be leaving the monastery today and needed to start packing. Maybe she would get some coffee from the common room while the others were in church. She had no intention of going anywhere near the weeping icon again. In fact, she couldn't wait to put as many miles as possible between herself and this place.

But as she walked down the hall toward the common room, she saw Katherine coming out of the workshop room, carrying her icon of Saint Mary of Egypt. Mare was embarrassed to be caught in her pajamas and robe; Katherine was fully dressed in a modest, long-sleeved blouse and ankle-length skirt. With her hair pulled underneath a scarf and her sensible, flat shoes, she reminded Mare of a librarian, or maybe a struggling housewife in a depression-era city.

Yet beauty radiated from her face.

"Are you going to bring your icon to be blessed this morning?" Katherine asked. Her question was innocent enough—she knew nothing about what had happened to Mare in the past twenty-four hours.

"Um, no. Well ... I wasn't. I'm not really sure. I just got up. Haven't showered or packed, so I may not have time."

"Oh, Mare, you'll miss the celebration. Want me to take your icon to Father Mark? I'll be careful with it ..."

Katherine's sweetness was hard to resist, and Mare couldn't think of an easy way to decline her offer.

"Sure, I guess so. Thanks."

She stepped into the workshop room, Katherine right behind, and walked over to the work table. She removed the cover on the icon of Archangel Michael and tested the oil to be sure it was dry. The icon had taken on a richness, the colors deepened by the oil. Mare was struck by its beauty, even if she had painted it herself. She handed the icon to Katherine.

"Wow, Mare. This is a really good first icon. I hope you'll come back—I mean it. Maybe you can do an icon of Saint Mary next time."

Mare smiled in spite of herself. "Thanks, Katherine, but I think I'm done with icons and monasteries. I'm headed back to

SCAD to finish school. I've had more than enough religion for a while."

Katherine's smile faded and her eyebrows came together. "What's going on, Mare?"

"Oh, nothing. You wouldn't understand. My life—oh, never mind. Just take the icon to Father Mark, okay?"

Katherine started to leave the room but paused at the door. "Mare, I come to this monastery because I was molested by my grandfather. It's taken me years to forgive him and allow God to begin to heal me. Saint Mary of Egypt helped."

Mare was stunned. *Why would she tell me this?* Standing at the table they had shared this week, painting icons together, she remembered Katherine's encouraging words—and her ready smile. She looked up from the table just as Katherine started out the door for the chapel.

"Wait. Please?" Mare whispered. "I had no idea."

Katherine, turned, crossed the room, and set the icons back down on the table. "Of course not. I hate to talk about it. Mother Christina knows, and she keeps encouraging me to come back to the icon workshop each year. It's been my therapy. Anyway, I'd better head to church and take our icons to be blessed. Will I see you at lunch?"

"Sure. Thanks."

"Is it okay if I hug you?"

The edges around Mare's emotions started to blur. Or maybe it was the way Katherine's face looked through the tears she was fighting back—fragile, yet strong, like fine porcelain that had been fired in a kiln. Mare responded by leaning into Katherine's arms. She pulled away after a moment and their eyes met. Then Katherine smiled, picked up the icons, and hurried out the door to the chapel.

Shit. Just when I was hoping to make a clean escape.

Mare's heart began to tug at her. Maybe she would just

go by the chapel briefly, after she was packed. She showered quickly, pulled on the only skirt she owned, threw the rest of her stuff into her suitcase, and scrounged around for the scarf she wore to that first service. Her only pair of socks was dirty, so she pulled on her sandals, hoping her bare feet and ankles wouldn't scandalize anyone. She had no intention of going to the front of the chapel and venerating that icon again. That was for damn sure.

Maybe no one would notice if she slipped in late and stood in the back.

• • •

Mare was surprised by the brightness of the chapel. Dozens of tapers filled the candle stands in front of the icons of Christ and the Mother of God. Even more surrounded the icon of Saint Mary of Egypt—*the one my mother painted*—in the middle of the nave. Flowers were everywhere; the strange aroma of incense and beeswax blended with their sweetness.

Visitors crowded the chapel, making it difficult for Mare to find a place to sit. The last people to be served communion were returning to their seats, each carefully cradling pieces of blessed bread in their hands. Katherine came over, offering a piece of bread, and stood beside her. She held their icons, one in each hand.

"Has he blessed them yet?" Mare whispered.

Katherine shook her head just before Father Mark's voice filled the chapel.

"We have just celebrated a glorious feast, thanks be to God," he said. "And now, if Sister Gabriella will assist me, I will bless the icons that were written by the workshop students this week. Will the students please come forward with their icons?"

Mare's heart sank. She hadn't planned on participating in a religious ceremony—she felt that simply being here was enough.

Katherine, apparently seeing her reaction, leaned down and whispered.

"It's okay, Mare. I'll take your icon up there."

"Thank you."

Katherine walked up front with the other students, forming a semi-circle around the weeping icon of Saint Mary. She still held both her own icon and Mare's, and Mare thought for an instant about sneaking out. Then she spotted Elaine, who was standing on the other side of the nave. Now Mare couldn't leave—she'd promised Elaine she would attend, and Elaine, from where she was standing, would see Mare depart the chapel. Mare turned back to Katherine and almost gasped aloud when Katherine nearly dropped her Archangel Michael icon. Elaine, moving quickly, joined Katherine and took the icon—Mare could see Elaine whisper something and offer what looked like a friendly smile. Katherine looked across the rows of visitors and found Mare. Her expression was full of apology, and Mare smiled at her.

Sister Susannah, Mare realized then, was chanting the hymns to Saint Mary of Egypt. It was an experience to hear her after learning that the reclusive nun was her *mother*. The other nuns joined her on the refrains, and the music continued as Father Mark took a brush and dipped it into the container that collected the tears from the weeping icon. Then he approached each student and sprinkled her icon with holy water that was mixed with the holy oil. His smooth voice filled the chapel:

"Send forth Your blessing upon this icon. Bless and make holy this Icon unto Your glory, in remembrance of You. Grant that this sanctification will be to all who venerate this icon and send up their prayers unto You. Through the grace and bounties and love of Your Only-Begotten Son, with Whom You are blessed, together with Your All-Holy, Good and Life-creating Spirit; both now and ever, and unto ages of ages. Amen."

What he did next caught Mare by surprise.

"And now, I would ask that each of the students remain here in front with their icons," he said. "As each of you comes forward to receive the blessing of the priest, you may also kiss each of these newly-blessed icons, which are worthy of veneration."

What? People kissing something I painted?

Suddenly Elaine was motioning for her to come hold her icon. All Mare could think about was the nausea rising in her throat—she could barely breathe. Her feet felt glued to the floor as the nuns—followed by the visitors—went forward to venerate the icons and receive the priest's blessing. All the while, Sister Susannah continued to chant in the background.

Then one of the visitors spoke up, her voice carrying the room:

"Father! Look! The icon has stopped weeping!"

Sister Susannah stopped chanting. Everyone stood while Father Mark went forward to look at the icon of Saint Mary of Egypt. Mother Christina and Sister Gabriella and the other nuns gathered around him, all waiting for the next drop of myrrh to fall from her eyes. Mare shook her head hard, trying desperately to clear it—despite her physical discomfort, she knew enough to understand that she was witnessing something remarkable. After a few moments, Father Mark instructed the nuns to continue singing.

"We will wait and watch," he said simply.

Another visitor raised her hand. "What does it mean, Father?"

"I do not know. Let us watch and pray. God will reveal His grace to us, just as He has done through the icon's weeping." Then he prostrated himself in front of the icon. All of the visitors and nuns knelt and bowed their heads and waited.

By now Mare was the lone person standing. With everyone kneeling, nothing obstructed her view of the icon. She, too, could see that no tears were falling from Saint Mary's eyes. Across the bowed heads of the worshippers she saw Sister Susannah, who walked away from the readers' stand ... and crossed the chapel toward Mare.

Mare felt herself freeze.

The images of the white-tailed deer flashed through her mind. Before she could tell her feet what to do, her mother's hand reached out to hold her own. Then Mare felt herself being pulled toward the center of the nave. As they walked toward the icon, Father Mark and Mother Christina stepped back, making way. Then Mare surprised herself by joining Sister Susannah on her knees in front of the icon, remaining there beside her mother.

Elaine joined them next, bringing Mare's icon with her and placing it in her hands. Mare looked at Elaine, thinking back for some reason to the opera and the way Elaine had taken her hand afterward. And then she looked at Sister Susannah, who in that moment seemed just as honest and genuine as Mother Christina, and something seemed to shift inside her. Then they were embracing—Mare, her mother, and her grandmother—and Mare gave voice through their intertwined bodies to something she wouldn't have been able to imagine saying last night.

"I forgive you. Both of you."

Mare's voice wasn't much above a whisper, but Father Mark rose from his knees and faced the nuns and visitors.

"We have witnessed a different kind of miracle here today," he said. "The icon of Saint Mary is no longer weeping; not because she is withdrawing her grace from us, but because the sadness that caused Saint Mary's weeping has *ceased*. Do not be disturbed by the cessation of her tears—but rather rejoice that these mothers and daughters, all victims of abuse and abandonment, have reconciled with one another today. The enemy no longer has power over them. Let us continue the Feast Day celebration with a special meal in the refectory."

• • •

The air outside the chapel seemed charged with more electricity than usual, and it seemed fresher, the way it was after a spring rain. The birds were singing louder. Trees swayed rhythmically in the breeze. Nuns and visitors alike moved with lightness as they went about their tasks or waited for the bell to ring for the noon meal.

"Uh, what just happened?" Mare asked Father Mark as they walked from the chapel to the refectory.

"A very unusual kind of miracle."

"So now I guess I'm expected to have some kind of miraculous conversion, right?"

"No one expects anything of you, Mare," he said reassuringly. "We are all rejoicing. You must decide how to proceed from here. Are you going back to SCAD with Elaine today?"

"Yeah. That's all I know for sure. I'll need some time to process all this. It's mind-boggling."

Sister Susannah and Elaine walked up to them. "Time for lunch," Sister Susannah said. "We've saved places at the head table for you two. Next to Father Mark."

Mare gave her mother a questioning look. "I thought that table was for priests and nuns."

Father Mark smiled. "On a day when a weeping icon stops weeping, on a day when three generations of women discover their shared history—the monastery can certainly bend its rules."

Mare smiled in spite of herself as she walked into the refectory, arm-in-arm with her mother and grandmother.

TWENTY-THREE

FIVE YEARS LATER

MARE FEARED THE worst when the phone rang and it was her mother.

"Mare?" Sister Susannah's voice was shaky. "You awake?"

"I am now." She reached for her bedside lamp and looked at the clock—five a.m. "Grandmother?"

"Yes, I'm afraid so. One of her friends called—she's back in the hospital. They're going to remove one of her lungs."

"Oh, damn." Mare pulled on her sweat pants and walked toward the kitchen, needing coffee. She eyed the pack of Camels on the counter and made a mental note to quit—again. She cursed internally when she found the Folgers canister empty, then picked up her smokes and headed for her third-floor walkup balcony.

"They won't know until they open her up and see if the cancer has spread. Either way, it's going to be rough."

"How's she holding up?"

"Pretty well. When we talked the other day, she was still on a high about her show at the Fischbach last month. I'm really thankful she got to do that. It'll probably be her swan song."

Elaine had visited Lascaux in southwestern France and painted a series she called the "Cave Paintings" just before her emphysema completely shut down her capacity to work.

"How quickly do you think we can get a flight to New York?"

"I'm going, but I think you should stay here. The exhibit opens in two days, and you've got a lot of work to do. You need to help the women at the shelter get ready."

Mare lit a cigarette and leaned on the balcony railing. The predawn darkness of downtown Atlanta offered little relief from the summer heat. A few people were stirring in the streets below, mostly homeless folks making their way to the breakfast lines at the mission. Her apartment was only a few blocks from the abused women's shelter that Sister Susannah ran—and where Mare volunteered as an art therapist.

"What about *your* work? Who's going to run the shelter while you're gone?"

"LadyP and the other employees and volunteers can take care of everything for a week or so. Elaine really needs me right now."

Sister Susannah, Mare knew, had never been able to bring herself to call Elaine "Mother," although Mare had taken to calling Sister Susannah "Mom" while still in school. It made her feel closer—like she belonged to someone. She finished her cigarette, stubbed it in an ashtray on the balcony, and went back inside.

"Do you need money for the flight?"

"No, thanks. Father Mark says I can use funds from the special account at St. Mary's. At first I felt bad about that, but he says it's for nuns like me who work in the world."

Mare was glad when her mother decided to leave the

monastery and move with her to Atlanta after Mare graduated from SCAD. She was even more pleased with Sister Susannah's decision to open the shelter. LadyP heard about the plans and applied for a job there; Father Mark and his parishioners were big supporters. As many as twenty-five women and children lived in the shelter these days, and Mare had taken a job waiting tables to supplement the income from her art sales. She spent a couple of mornings a week helping the women at the shelter work through their abuse issues by drawing or painting. The studio that showed Mare's work had agreed to sponsor a show for the women from the shelter—all proceeds would go toward the purchase of playground equipment for the children who stayed there.

"Okay. I'll take care of everything here. Do what you need to for Grandmother, and let me know you're there safely, okay?"

Grandmother. It had become a term of endearment over the last five years, defining the nature of their relationship. Mare had also discovered a measure of compassion for Elaine. After all, without her she might never have found her mother. Or her true calling, abstract expressionism and art therapy.

The women at the shelter, who were blessed with talent and resilience, were eager to share their stories (including LadyP, with whom Mare and Sister Susannah had developed a strong bond). Mare gave the women the opportunity they needed—free art classes on Tuesdays and Thursdays—and the rest was up to them. Some, like LadyP, chose to accompany Mare on *legal* throwups, expressing themselves through graffiti at sanctioned sites around town. Others at the shelter chose a more traditional route, working through their issues on canvas or watercolor paper. One recent student, a young woman from Alabama who had been molested by a member of a cult-like home church, had asked for Mare's help with an icon.

"Why do you want to do an icon, Sarah?" Mare was curious

about her interest in a liturgical art form barely known outside of the Orthodox and Catholic churches, especially in the South.

"This group I was with," Sarah said, "we were studying the history of the Church. Before I left we learned about icons. About Saint Mary of Egypt. I'd really like to paint her."

Mare remembered Sister Gabriella's reasons for not letting a new student do an icon of this particular saint at the monastery workshop. Surely the rules didn't apply to the street ministry her mother had established here in Atlanta, though, or to the art classes she herself led. These women were struggling to regain their self-worth. They needed affirmation, not rules. Freedom, not constraint.

"That's a wonderful idea. I have a sketch that might help you get started."

The shelter's show would be part of the Atlanta neighborhood association's monthly art walk. The students were afraid that people would not venture into their neighborhood without police protection, so Mare had secured a section of an upscale gallery in a better part of town that showed her work regularly. A dozen or so women were contributing to the show—everything from rough charcoal sketches to watercolor and gouache to graffiti. Even a Coptic-style icon of Saint Mary of Egypt.

• • •

Mare had arranged for Lou Lieberman to come to Atlanta to photograph the graffiti pieces for the exhibit, which added considerable marketing value to the event. Lou had left *Rolling Stone,* and her work had garnered many national awards since Mare met her back in Macon. Lou had also worked with LadyP on a shoot of her recent work on warehouse walls, and the plan was for her to bring her photographs to the show, where they would join works in other media on the gallery walls. Mare felt a surge of pride as she dressed to meet Lou at Pryor, where some of her own paintings had been shown recently.

Dressed in black ankle pants and a white, off-the-shoulder knit top, Mare was hardly the teenager she'd been back at SCAD. Heels replaced her canvas tennis shoes, and her hair fell in soft curls on her shoulders. A silver pendant in the shape of a heart—a gift from Elaine last Christmas—hung down to the top of a hint of cleavage. She greeted Lou at the back door of the gallery a couple of hours before the show to help hang the photographs.

"Wow." Lou almost dropped an armful of images as she entered and saw Mare. "Somebody grew up. What are you now, twenty-one?"

"Twenty-two, actually." Mare smiled as she helped Lou carry the photos to a table in front of a nearby wall. "Here, I reserved this area for your prints. Hope there's enough room."

"Looks perfect." Lou stepped back from the table and eyed the space. Then she turned back to Mare. "I am *so* damn proud of you." They embraced, and Mare remembered the first time Lou had hugged her, back in her apartment in Macon.

"Thanks. And thanks for doing this for us," Mare replied. "I remember how it felt to be powerless, to be invisible. I wanted to give these women a place where their voices could be heard, where they could be seen through their art."

"I'm so impressed. The pieces I photographed over on those warehouse walls were amazing. Come on, help me hang them."

Mare and Lou labeled each piece with white placards that displayed the name of each artist and the cost.

"You sure you're okay donating these?" Mare asked. "You could have made a lot of money off them."

Lou smiled. "Some things are more important than money."

• • •

Finally it was time for the show. Father Mark and a few more supporters from St. Mary's were already there. Many regular customers showed up, eager to support the shelter's residents. Soon the gallery was brimming with an unlikely mixture of graffiti writers, homeless women, and well-to-do art patrons. Mare took a long look around and kept an ear on conversations that were taking place. The attendees were sipping wine together, strange bedfellows united by their passion for art.

"Oh, I love this one!" a tall, slim woman exclaimed to her husband as they approached a large abstract piece in the front room of the gallery. The objects in the painting—a house, a tree, a swing set, and a car—were represented in sepia and white but with the colors inverted, like an old photograph negative. A young female artist stood nearby, fingering her program nervously as the couple approached. "Is this yours?"

"Yes, ma'am."

"Is this your house, in the painting?"

"Oh, no, ma'am. I ain't got no house. It's just something I dream about. That's why I painted it that way. Like a picture that ain't been developed yet, you know?"

Mare, twenty feet away, smiled when the woman wrote a check for $250 and one of the volunteers put a red dot on the painting—sold. Just then she spotted a young man entering the room in the gallery where Lou's photographs of two shelter artists' graffiti pieces were displayed. Mare walked in, greeted him, and introduced him to the two artists.

"Wow, I wouldn't have thought women did this sort of thing," he said. He smiled and shook the hands of the two women—the shorter of whom was LadyP.

"We wouldn't have had the courage to throw our stuff up without Mare's help," she said.

"This is Anne Louise Lieberman," Mare replied, not wanting to call attention to herself. "She did the photography for these pieces."

"Lou Lieberman? *The* Lou Lieberman?"

"Pleased to meet you," Lou replied, and shook the man's hand. "It was easy. Their pieces are amazing. The show is about them, not me."

The man brought out his checkbook. Mare caught LadyP's eye and winked as another red dot was attached to a frame on the gallery wall. Then a volunteer tugged on Mare's arm.

"Excuse me, Mare," she said, and nodded apologetically to the patron, Lou, and LadyP. A grim expression was on the volunteer's face—and Mare knew what was coming. "It's your mother on the phone. Said it's urgent."

Mare quickly followed the volunteer to the office in the back of the gallery and picked up the phone receiver. The volunteer walked out, pulling the door closed behind her.

"Mom?"

"Mare. How's the show going?"

"Amazing. Most of the pieces have sold already—how's Grandmother?"

Sister Susannah sighed. "She didn't survive the surgery. We lost her this afternoon. I hate to cast a dark cloud over such a happy event, but I knew you'd want to know."

For some reason, the news took Mare back to that evening at the monastery when Sister Christina and Father Mark had arranged for Elaine and the mysterious Sister Susannah to talk—it seemed to Mare that everyone was in on a bunch of secrets except her, and she felt left out. It was almost like that now, even though she'd agreed to stay in Atlanta while her mother went to New York.

"Why didn't you call earlier?"

"Because, honey, I knew she would want the exhibit to go on."

"I'm sure you're right. I'll be on the first plane tomorrow morning."

"Good. Please tell Father Mark. He might want to come, too.

Now, enjoy the rest of the evening. Elaine would have wanted it that way."

Mare told her mother that she loved her, then hung up and returned to the show and found Father Mark in a state of excitement.

"There you are, Mare. Come look!"

He led Mare to the front of the gallery, where Sarah's icon of Saint Mary of Egypt was on display and the gallery patrons and a group of artists from the shelter were crowding around it. The artist, Sarah, was on her knees in front of the icon, crying.

Drops of oil were falling from the eyes of the saint onto the floor of the gallery.

Sarah looked up at Father Mark and Mare as they entered the room. "What—what does it mean, Father?"

Father Mark stared at the icon for a moment. "I'm not sure yet," he said to Sarah. Then he looked up. "Let's all watch and be still a few minutes."

The gathering, despite the priest's request for quiet, began to murmur. Some crowded in for a closer look. Mare cleared her throat.

"Elaine de Kooning died today. A terrific artist," she said in a hoarse whisper. "She was also my grandmother. And my teacher."

The group fell silent. Father Mark, standing next to Mare, made the sign of the cross before giving her a fatherly hug. Everyone remained quiet, even the patrons who began to leave, and the gallery owner who had been watching the whole scene. Finally Sarah broke the silence.

"What's going to happen to my icon?"

"If you don't mind, it really belongs in a church," Father Mark said. "And I need to call a bishop to come and validate the miracle."

Sarah looked crestfallen. Mare stepped over to her and asked what was wrong.

"It's just that ... this is the best thing that's ever happened to me. I don't want anyone to take it away."

Father Mark motioned for Sarah and Mare to join him in some nearby chairs. Several folks who were still left joined them, including Lou and LadyP. Once they were seated, he continued.

"You see, a weeping icon is a gift to be shared with others," he said to Sarah. "If you take it back to the shelter with you—or even to an apartment—no one else will be able to receive its blessing. At a church, though, many people can come and pray before it and ask Saint Mary for comfort. Does that make sense?"

Sarah, still crying, looked up and nodded briefly.

"Father?" Mare asked. "Can we take it back to the shelter just for tonight, and you can call the bishop tomorrow?"

"That would be fine, so long as the icon is treated with reverence at the shelter. May I go with you to set up a temporary place for it?"

"Absolutely," Mare said. She helped Sarah to her feet and hugged her. Lou went with them, and Father Mark arrived soon after, bringing a small pottery bowl, sand, and candles. Mare and Sarah helped him choose a place to set up the icon on a small easel. Father Mark then placed a container at the base to collect the oil that continued to drip from the icon. Lou photographed the whole scene—the weeping icon with Mare and Father Mark and Sarah sitting reverently in front of it.

Then Lou put her camera down and reached for a candle. She lit it and put it next to the others in the sand.

AUTHOR'S NOTE

A work of historical fiction is sometimes described as a narrative that takes place in the past in which historical events and people are reconstructed to enhance the story. *Cherry Bomb* isn't strictly a work of historical fiction, for several reasons. For one thing, I have fictionalized the lives of several abstract expressionist artists, especially Elaine de Kooning, who plays a major role in the book. While many of the scenarios in which de Kooning appears in the book were taken from her actual life—her relationship from childhood with her eccentric mother; her early art education in New York; her marriage to Willem de Kooning; and even some of her travels—I have also fictionalized many aspects of her real life. Perhaps the greatest liberty I took was giving her a child, when in fact she never had children of her own.

While Elaine de Kooning did paint a presidential portrait of John F. Kennedy, as I describe in the book, she was never a visiting professor at Southern College of Art and Design, although she did serve this post at the University of Georgia. She did spend a summer painting in Black Mountain, North Carolina, and produced a collection of work from that experience, although in reality Willem was there with her—whereas she goes there without him in the book. These are examples of ways in which I fictionalized her life for the sake of the storyline.

The photographer Anne Louise Lieberman ("Lou") and Margaret Adams, the newspaper reporter, are completely fictional characters, as are the graffiti writers Mare meets in Atlanta. But the scenes in the MTV video with the rock band Blondie actually did show the work of graffiti artists Lee Quinones and Jean-Michael Basquiat, who inspire Mare to begin doing graffiti.

I set *Cherry Bomb* mostly in the 1980s, with flashbacks to de Kooning's childhood in the 1930s and the childhood of the fictional protagonist, Mary Catherine Henry ("Mare"), in the 1970s. Mare is a completely fictional character, as is Sister Susannah, an Orthodox nun and iconographer who also plays a major role in the story. Both priests—Father Joseph and Father Mark—are completely fictional, as are all the nuns and participants at the icon workshop at Saint Mary of Egypt Monastery (also a fictional place).

Saint Mary of Egypt is an actual historical figure, and I have kept close to the facts of her life as the Orthodox priest, Father Mark, relates and explains them in the book. The verses chanted by the nuns at the monastery are closely drawn from her life as documented by Saint Sophronius, Patriarch of Jerusalem (634-638 A.D.). It might be of interest to the reader that Sir John Tavener did write an opera about Mary of Egypt—although he wrote it in 1991, a little later than its placement in the book. The description of the opera in the book is taken from a program from one of its performances. While I haven't seen the opera in person, I do have Tavener's CD, *Mary of Egypt*, which I have listened to many times.

Of course readers often ask whether a work of fiction is in any way autobiographical. While it is true that I share a number of life experiences with Mare—including time spent with a cult-like group, sexual abuse, and studying iconography at an Orthodox monastery—I have only allowed those experiences to inform the narrative, which means it is *not* a fictionalized memoir. I have never lived in a foster home, thrown up graffiti in public places, studied at SCAD, or met Elaine de Kooning. But I am happy for my readers to know that I am a convert to Orthodox Christianity, that I have personally witnessed weeping icons, and that Mary of Egypt is my patron saint. Holy Mother Mary, pray to God for us.